He was anything but predictable

Jeff was going to ask her out—Autumn just knew it. She fidgeted, waiting for the expected invitation.

"Autumn, I want to talk to you about something."

Here it comes. "Yes?"

"I'm considering installing new outdoor lighting, particularly around the pool. What would you recommend?"

Outdoor lighting? Was he serious? "I'd have to see the pool before I could recommend anything," she answered, surprised by the sharpness of her disappointment.

"Of course. I'll call your company and try to schedule time with you."

"Fine." She was itching to engage Jeff in a searing kiss like the one he'd given her the last time they'd met. Instead, she muttered, "I, um, I guess I'll see you later, then."

Jeff held the door for her. As she stepped through, he said softly in her ear, "You know, this could go on a long time. Until I run out of electrical ideas. Or money." Before she could answer, he had closed the door quietly in her face.

Gina Wilkins has done it again with this third book in her delightful trilogy about the three Reed sisters from Rose Bud, Arkansas. Be prepared for the sparks that fly between the youngest sister, Autumn, and Jeff Bradford. Gina says she had plenty of technical advice about her heroine's profession from the four electricians in her family—her father and three brothers—who all confessed they enjoyed reading this romance novel.

Gina and her husband live with their two daughters in Jacksonville, Arkansas.

Books by Gina Wilkins

HARLEQUIN TEMPTATION
174–HERO IN DISGUISE
198–HERO FOR THE ASKING

Hero by Nature

GINA WILKINS

Harlequin Books

TORONTO • NEW YORK • LONDON
AMSTERDAM • PARIS • SYDNEY • HAMBURG
STOCKHOLM • ATHENS • TOKYO • MILAN

For my favorite electricians—
Vernon Vaughan, my father,
and my brothers, Dennis, Pat and Doug.
Thanks, guys.

Published May 1988

ISBN 0-373-25304-4

1

AUTUMN REED HOPPED nimbly out of the cab of the pickup, tugging the brim of her battered brown baseball cap low over her oversized sunglasses to shade her face from the afternoon sun. Her auburn hair was looped into a French braid, which had loosened over the course of the day so that it bobbed behind her as she strode briskly toward the front door of the impressively sized ranch-style house to which she'd been dispatched. To anyone reading body language, her movements were indicative of her personality—quick, restless, energetic, no-nonsense. She punched the doorbell with a slender, short-nailed finger, then waited impatiently for a response.

"Well, hell," she muttered when there was no sound of a chime inside to announce her arrival. The electricity was out. What was she doing ringing the bell? She knocked loudly, imperatively.

While she waited for the door to open, she looked around. The house was gorgeous, the lawn beautifully landscaped. But then it had to be, in this Tampa, Florida neighborhood of equally gorgeous homes, equally beautiful lawns.

The door opened, bringing her shaded green eyes back around. The man in the doorway was as beautiful as his home, she thought with detached amusement. Young, probably early thirties. Coal-black hair brushed casually back from a tanned, classically

handsome face. Perfectly arched black brows over deep
blue eyes, perfectly straight nose, perfectly even white
teeth exposed by a mouth shaped for fantasies. Smooth,
dimpled cheeks, square jaw, six feet plus of body that
could serve as an advertisement for a health spa. He
was one of your finer examples of the human male, and
Autumn was woman enough to react quite physically.
Mentally she knew that there had to be more to a man
than a pretty face to make him worth her interest.

"I'm with Brothers Electrical Company. You called
for an electrician?" she asked in her direct, uncere-
monious manner.

"Well, yes, but . . ." He paused, looking at her with a
doubtful frown.

She sighed resignedly. Damn. One of those. "I am a
licensed electrician," she assured him in a bored voice.
"If you need to check me out, call the office. Of course,
I charge by the hour and you're wasting time."

"I'm sorry," the attractive man answered, visibly
flustered. "I wasn't questioning your competence. I was
simply surprised that you're a . . ." His voice trailed off
again.

"Woman." A very nice voice, Autumn thought automatically, even as she supplied the word for him.
Low, rich, unapologetically Southern. Classy, too. Like
someone who was intelligent and well educated but
didn't feel the need to make a big deal out of it. She had
a habit of summing people up within a few minutes of
making their acquaintance. She typed this guy as a
successful professional with impeccable manners and
a deeply ingrained woman's-place-is-in-the-kitchen-
and-bedroom mentality. Too bad. "What's your problem?" she asked briskly.

"I beg your— Oh, you mean why did I call an electrician," he stammered, his eyes never leaving her face, or at least that part of it visible beneath her cap and huge sunglasses. Autumn wondered if she had overestimated his intelligence. "It's the box on the side of the house, the one by the electric meter," he told her finally, after clearing his throat. "A limb blew down during the thunderstorm last night and knocked it almost completely off. The electric company disconnected my power but told me I'd have to call an electrician to reinstall the service."

Autumn nodded. "No problem. I'll get my tools, then you can show me where it is." She whirled and headed back to the black Ford Ranger with the magnetic signs advertising the name of the company she worked for. Her belt was in the cab, and she retrieved that first. She strapped the tools around her slender waist, over her khaki jumpsuit, seemingly oblivious to the fact that the heavy tool pouch added almost fifteen pounds to her usual one hundred and ten. Then she reached into the bed of the truck for her ladder and toolbox, only to stop short when a long, tanned arm reached past hers.

"I'll carry those for you," the dark-haired man offered, muscles rippling as he lifted out the heavy red metal toolbox as if it weighed practically nothing.

Begrudging him his superior strength, Autumn tried to protest when he reached back in for the fiberglass ladder. "I can get it. I'm used to carrying my own tools."

"No trouble at all," the man assured her, already moving away, toolbox in one hand and ladder balanced over his other shoulder, giving her a very nice view of his muscular back and lean hips. "This way, Miss...?"

She exhaled impatiently and followed him. "Just call me Autumn," she told him.

"Autumn," he repeated solemnly, smiling around at her. "That's a very pretty name."

"Thanks," she answered briskly, uncomfortable with the compliment.

"I'm Jeff Bradford. And here's the reason I called you."

Autumn raised one dark eyebrow at the sight he indicated. He hadn't exaggerated. His service entrance was almost completely torn off the house, though fortunately it hadn't been badly damaged. That would save her a trip after a new box. She pulled a screwdriver out of her pouch. "This is going to take a couple of hours," she informed him. "I'll try to have your electricity back on by late afternoon."

"I'd appreciate it," he responded with a charming smile.

Autumn swallowed and turned to her ladder. Lord, but he was attractive! Distracting, as well. "I'll let you know when I'm finished," she told him in what she hoped was a dismissive tone.

"I think I'll watch, if you don't mind," he replied diffidently. "It's, uh, it's dark in the house, and I've nothing better to do."

She shrugged, determined not to show him that his magnificent presence was in any way disconcerting. "Suit yourself." She tossed out the words and set to work with grim concentration.

Jeff shoved his fingertips into the pockets of his gray denim jeans and leaned one shoulder against the side of his house as he watched her climb three rungs of the ladder. The siding was rough through his thin cotton knit shirt, but he spared the sensation little thought as he mentally castigated himself. He was acting like a tongue-tied idiot, he told himself with disgust. What on earth had gotten into him? Fifteen minutes earlier he'd been a fairly bright, reasonably urbane kind of guy, and then he'd opened his door to this woman and lost whatever intelligence he may have possessed. He hadn't said anything worth listening to since she'd first spoken to him in that low, husky voice.

And the hell of it was, he wasn't even sure if he found her all that attractive. Her hair was a pretty color, kind of a dark red as best he could tell from the functional braid. Her face was almost completely hidden by that beat-up baseball cap and those ridiculous sunglasses. What he could see was very nice. Small nose, squarish cheeks, soft, sensually shaped mouth that did not owe its rosy color to cosmetic aid. She was small, the top of her head coming just to his chin—about five, five he guessed. As for her figure, it might be good, but who could tell with that loose-fitting jumpsuit and bulky tool pouch? And even if a woman like this would deign to enter a beauty pageant, she certainly wouldn't win the prize for Miss Congeniality. So why had he suddenly developed a tendency to stutter?

He reached up automatically to take the metal box she'd just disconnected, noting the slight twist of her mouth as he did so. She wasn't overly pleased about him helping her. One of those rabid feminists who entered a vocation normally filled by men, then found it necessary to continually justify her choice, he decided. Well, he was sure she was a fine electrician and he couldn't care less if she chose to spend her time twisting wires, though he couldn't imagine why anyone would want to do so. Personally, he preferred women who were softer, more feminine, whatever their chosen careers. Less antagonistic.

Then she tugged off her sunglasses and shoved them into the breast pocket of her jumpsuit, glancing down at him as she did so. Jeff froze, staring at her like the tongue-tied idiot he'd just accused himself of being.

He'd always heard that one could tell a sorceress by her eyes.

Green. The truest green he'd ever seen, with deep, hot flames, carefully banked, in their depths. Evidence of a fiery temper, he was sure. He found himself wondering if her passion was as volatile. He would be willing to bet it was. Her long eyelashes and boldly shaped eyebrows were unusually dark in combination with her auburn hair.

She was beautiful. He'd suspected that she was attractive, but he hadn't guessed that there was a rare, earthy beauty hidden behind those god-awful dark glasses. And he was standing there like a tourist gazing in awe at the Statue of Liberty.

Make conversation. "How long have you been an electrician?" he asked abruptly. *Oh, terrific line. Straight out of* How to Win Friends and Influence People, he thought with a mental groan.

Autumn glanced down from her work, intending to let him know that if he was going to stand there, she would appreciate it if he'd be quiet and let her work. Instead, she found herself staring at a generous, warm smile that only a coldhearted puppy hater could ignore. "Almost five years," she answered, her voice more friendly than she'd originally intended. She looked back at the mess of wires in front of her, trying to concentrate on what she was doing.

"Do you enjoy it?"

"Beats sitting behind a typewriter," she replied as she pulled a pair of side-cutting pliers from her pouch.

Her action drew Jeff's eyes back down to her waist, which was just below his eye level. He was suddenly fascinated by the roll of black electrician's tape that dangled from a chain on her belt, swaying against her hip as she moved. He cleared his throat and turned his eyes sternly upward. "You're not from Florida originally, are you?" he asked.

"No, Arkansas. Hand me that set of cable cutters out of my toolbox, will you?" Autumn decided that keeping him busy might just keep his mouth shut, though she doubted it. She thought he had a very nice voice, but it was definitely distracting.

Jeff frowned into the open toolbox, staring at the assortment of tools there. The only thing he recognized was a big screwdriver. He'd never been much of a handyman—by choice. He preferred to pay people to do that sort of thing. Now he wished he hadn't chosen extra science classes over shop. Using a rapid process of elimination, he grabbed something big and heavy and held it up. "You mean this?"

"Yeah, thanks," she said casually, taking the tool from him and turning back to the service.

He just managed not to say "whew" and wipe his brow. He didn't know why he was suddenly trying to impress this woman, but he felt as if he'd just earned himself a few points.

"Now would you hand me—"

Jeff tensed, glaring back down at the toolbox. *What now?*

"The hacksaw?" Autumn finished.

Thank goodness. Jeff snatched up the vaguely familiar instrument and offered it upward, grinning broadly.

Autumn took the saw, wondering why Jeff was suddenly looking so pleased with himself. Strange guy, she mused. Gorgeous but strange.

A particularly vigorous movement on her part shook the ladder beneath her, but Autumn wasn't concerned as she steadied herself on the wall in front of her. After all, her feet were barely three feet off the ground. She'd fallen farther.

Jeff, however, was not so unconcerned. He reached out at the first shimmy of the ladder and steadied her, one hand on the ladder, one on the back of her leg, a scant few inches below the slender curve of her hip.

"You okay?" he asked.

Impatient, she sighed and looked down. "Yes, I'm . . . fine." Her voice faded as she looked down into the face turned up to hers, their gazes locking. She was suddenly vividly aware of that warm hand on the back of her thigh. She cleared her throat soundlessly, "You want to, uh . . ."

"Do I want to what?" Jeff asked eagerly.

"You want to move your hand?" she continued more forcefully.

His mouth tilting into a one-sided smile that she secretly found devastating, he looked down the length of her body to the hand in question. "No, not particularly," he informed her.

"Well, do it, anyway," Autumn snapped. "I'm trying to work here."

"Sorry," he murmured, looking back up at her with sparkling blue eyes that showed not the faintest apology. He moved the hand but took his time about it.

Autumn tightened her jaw and turned curtly back to the job before her, telling herself that she was *not* blushing. Dammit, she hadn't blushed since junior-high school! What was with this guy, changing from a rather sweet, shy, awkward type to a practiced flirt in the blink of an eye?

Rebuilding Jeff Bradford's meter loop should have been a routine, if painstaking, job, requiring little more than perfunctory concentration on Autumn's part. In reality, it became a test of her skill and professionalism as she struggled grimly to perform her job while her uninvited "helper" hovered beneath her, making cheerful conversation, offering assistance when none was needed, occasionally handing her a tool in response to a grudging request. Autumn had to ask herself more than once why she was being so patient with him. She had been less patient with other pesky males, customer or not, and had even been known to lose her formidable temper with a few. But Jeff continued to be so relentlessly nice and courteous that she would have felt like a complete shrew had she been anything less than tolerant of him, though her tolerance may have been a bit forced.

"Do you know that you have the most beautiful eyes I've ever seen?" he asked her at one point, gazing earnestly up at her. "Are they naturally that green, or do you wear contacts?"

Autumn swallowed and dropped the stripping knife she'd been using, relieved that it fell nowhere near her uninvited assistant. "Jeff, do you suppose you could bring me a glass of water?" she asked with hidden desperation, unaware that she'd casually called him by his first name. "It's, uh, it's really hot out here."

He grinned, as aware as she that the moist, late-October breeze around them was quite comfortable. "Sure, Autumn," he answered without further comment. "I'll be right back."

"Don't hurry," she called after him.

The next four and a half minutes were the most peaceful time she'd managed since Jeff Bradford had answered her knock on his door. So why did she catch herself smiling when he returned with the requested water?

"Almost finished now," she announced a short while later, relieved that she'd done a creditable job despite her uncharacteristic clumsiness. "I just have to connect these grounding wires to the back of the box and—"

Because her attention was more on the man beside her than on what she was doing, she awkwardly allowed the screwdriver she was using to slip out of the groove of the screw, the forward momentum of her hand causing her knuckles to smash painfully into the side of the metal box. Autumn swore colorfully under her breath, jerking her abused hand out of the box. She was particularly chagrined that she had done this in front of Jeff, although it was a common occurrence in her job.

As she would have expected, he reacted with sympathy and concern. "Are you okay?" he demanded for the second time that afternoon. "Let me see your hand."

"It's fine, Jeff, really. I just—" Her words died in a resigned sigh as he took her slender hand in his bigger ones, probing and massaging with the skill of an expert.

"Nothing broken, but you're going to have some interesting bruises," Jeff told her with relief. "It will be sore. You really should wrap it in ice."

"Really, Jeff, it's okay. I've done this before. More often than I like to remember," she assured him, embarrassed. "Occupational hazard."

His thumb traced the delicate bones in her hand. "You've broken a couple of these bones, haven't you?" he asked, feeling the almost imperceptible ridges beneath her surprisingly soft skin.

"Yeah, I broke a couple of bones in an accident once. What are you . . . a doctor?"

"Pediatrician," he admitted.

She hadn't really thought he was a doctor. She'd only been asking to divert his attention from her hand. For some reason she was suddenly self-conscious, though she couldn't have explained why. "If you'll let go of my hand, I'll finish this up," she told him rather briskly.

"You're always asking me to let go just when I'd like to hold on," Jeff complained good-naturedly, though he released her hand.

Autumn made a concerted effort to ignore him as she rapidly completed her job and climbed down the ladder—with Jeff's help, of course. She figured that his mother must have taken him to classes in Southern gallantry from the time he could walk. She tried to tell herself that his studious politeness annoyed her, even as she found herself thanking him for his assistance. What on earth was wrong with her?

Her tools packed neatly into the truck, she turned to him with a work order on a clipboard. "Just sign right here, Dr. Bradford, and you'll be billed for the service. You can call the electric company now and have your power turned back on."

"Dr. Bradford?" he quizzed her as he signed the work order in an illegible scrawl that befitted his occupation. Autumn had never met a doctor who could write anything readable. "You called me Jeff earlier."

"Did I?" she murmured vaguely. "Well, goodbye. Thank you for calling Brothers Electrical Company. Give us a call if you need anything else." Her customary recitation concluded, she turned to the truck, intending to leave without further delay.

Jeff, however, had different intentions. "Will you have dinner with me this evening?" he asked her, surprising them both. He hadn't intended to ask quite so abruptly—he wasn't even free that evening, he remembered wryly—but when she'd started walking away with such finality, he'd spoken almost without thinking. Now he decided that if she accepted, he'd just call Julian, his partner and buddy, and cancel out on the poker game. Julian would understand. Jeff really wanted a chance to get to know this interesting woman. There was just something about her that he found fascinating.

Autumn wasn't particularly surprised that he'd asked. Not after the past couple of hours. What *did* surprise her was that she found herself suddenly tempted to accept. Not that she had any intention of doing so. Something about Dr. Jeff Bradford made her nervous, somewhat unsure of herself, and Autumn Reed wasn't accustomed to such feelings. Above all, she liked being firmly in control of herself. No, Jeff was too overwhelmingly attractive, too unpredictably charming, too . . . well, too something. Besides, she already had a date that evening with a man who was amusing, attractive in a less spectacular way, and much more manageable. "Thank you for asking, but I already have plans," she told him after a brief pause, keeping her voice deliberately distant.

Jeff shrugged almost imperceptibly and backed off. "Maybe I'll see you around sometime," he told her.

"Maybe," Autumn agreed, climbing into the cab of the pickup. Her tone was not encouraging.

"Goodbye, Autumn."

"Bye, Jeff." She closed her door with a snap and drove away.

Some fifteen minutes later Jeff replaced the telephone in its cradle, having been assured that his power would be turned back on within the hour. He roamed aimlessly into his den, dropping moodily onto the heavy wood-framed couch, its deep cushions sinking beneath his weight. *So you struck out*, he told himself, disgruntled. It wasn't a first, though he couldn't actually remember the last time. Jeff was no womanizing playboy, but then, he'd never had much trouble getting a date, either. Of course, he rarely came across like a thick-skulled, inarticulate chauvinist, he added with an audible groan, sinking deeper into the couch cushions. No wonder Autumn had turned him down.

For all he knew, she was heavily involved with someone. She could even be married, though she hadn't worn a ring. But then, she hadn't worn any jewelry at all. *Forget her, Bradford*, he ordered himself sternly. *She's just not interested.*

He shoved himself off the couch, determined to do just that.

JEFF WASN'T GRINNING when he opened his door two weeks later, but Autumn suspected that he was holding it back only with tremendous effort. "You called for an electrician?" she asked him coolly, eyeing him with suspicion.

"As a matter of fact, I did," he replied, just a bit smugly. "Please come in."

Her suspicions increased. "First tell me what you need done so I'll know what tools to bring."

"I need an additional outlet in my den," he informed her.

She repressed a sigh and nodded. "Okay. Hang on a minute." She turned abruptly and headed back to her truck.

Jeff followed, of course, and had her toolbox out before she could even reach for it. She totally ignored him. Outwardly, at least. Inwardly, she was vitally aware of every inch of him in his thin blue sweater, which hugged his torso and made his eyes look even bluer, and his slim-cut jeans that left little to her imagination. She hadn't forgotten the effect he had on her. Which was why she intended to stay well over an arm's length away from him while she finished this job in record time.

Autumn tried not to look impressed by the interior of Jeff's house, but it wasn't easy. It was beautiful. Professionally decorated, she was sure, but comfortable and inviting. He'd chosen to ignore the usual wicker-and-palm-tree or pseudo-Spanish styles popular in the area and had decorated in a rustic Southwestern theme. Autumn recognized the many examples of Seminole artwork scattered with studied casualness throughout the house. The Seminole Culture Center on Orient Road had been one of the first sights she'd visited after moving to Tampa almost a year earlier.

"This is where I'd like the outlet," Jeff told her, indicating a section of white-painted Sheetrock wall in his den.

She studied the wall. "No problem, but you have a receptacle just a few feet away from there," she pointed out.

"It's not convenient. To plug in the vacuum cleaner I have to crawl behind that chair," he replied.

Plug in the vacuum cleaner? She wondered how often he performed that particular operation himself. "You could move the chair."

"I like it where it is," he answered with a bland smile. "Do you want the job or not, Autumn?"

She shrugged. "It's your money." Frowning, she examined the grin that had finally broken across his gorgeous face. "I suppose you want to watch me work?"

"If you don't mind."

As if it mattered whether she minded or not. She sighed and tried one more ploy to get him a bit farther away from her. "Don't you doctors ever work?"

"Thursday's my day off," he answered genially.

"Then your meter loop was blown off on a convenient day, wasn't it?" she murmured, remembering that she had met him on a Thursday. Two weeks ago today, she thought. She refused to dwell on how often she had thought of him during those two weeks.

He shrugged, an obvious imitation of her. Autumn glared at him and started to work.

It was the last time all over again. Jeff hovered around her, helping whenever she'd let him, chatting with her whenever she'd bother to answer. It was apparent that he was going out of his way to charm her. And, dammit, she thought glumly, after he'd unexpectedly made her laugh out loud at one of his quips, he was doing it. She found she had a definite weakness for Dr. Jeff Bradford, a weakness that she had no intention of indulging. Despite his many attractions, she had learned her lesson about getting involved with charming, old-fashioned males. Five years earlier she'd broken her engagement to a very nice man who had tried and failed to break her rebellious spirit. She'd never regretted that decision.

"Almost finished," she announced, tightening the screws on the plastic outlet plate.

"This is going to be very handy. Thanks."

"You paid for it." She stashed the screwdriver in her pouch as she stood and pulled the hem of her jeans from behind the tab at the heel of her gray nylon-and-suede jogging shoes.

"How was your date?" Jeff asked unexpectedly.

Autumn lifted one dark eyebrow. "What date?"

"The one you turned me down for two weeks ago," he reminded her, watching her closely.

"Oh." She'd almost forgotten that date. It had been quite forgettable. She'd thought about Jeff all evening, which had not put her in the best of moods for the amusing, attractive and manageable man she'd been with. "It was fine."

"Will you go out with me tonight?" Jeff asked immediately.

She'd been expecting an invitation this time and had decided in advance that she was going to turn him down. But doing so was even harder than it had been the first time. Deep inside she liked Jeff Bradford. She knew she'd have a good time if she went out with him. She also knew that it would only take a touch from him to smash her normally formidable willpower into quivering blobs. And *that* was a dangerous, sobering realization. "I'm sorry. I can't."

"Tomorrow night?"

When had he moved so close to her? Autumn looked straight up into his eyes as she declined again. "No, I..." Since when had her voice ever been breathless and fluttery? she asked herself in disgust. She cleared her throat and spoke more firmly. "I can't."

He took another step forward. "Saturday?"

There seemed to be a short developing in her breathing apparatus. Her breath was coming in uneven little jerks, growing worse in direct proportion to Jeff's increasing proximity. She swallowed and stepped back, only to find herself backed against the arm of the massive chair they had discussed earlier. "No, thank you," she managed.

"Should I keep asking?" he inquired gently, lifting his hands to take her by the forearms, steadying her when she would have stumbled against the chair.

"No, you...you needn't bother," Autumn answered with a firmness she found somewhere deep inside her. Finding his bright blue eyes too mesmerizing, she dropped her own gaze to his chest, only to find herself staring in admiration at the glistening V of tanned skin exposed by the neckline of his sweater. A nest of dark curls lay there, looking soft and all too tempting.

"Is there someone else?" Jeff persisted, bringing her face back up to his by way of a gently insistent hand beneath her chin.

Becoming annoyed, she lifted her chin further to avoid his hand. "There's not anyone else specifically. I'm just not interested in going out with you, Jeff."

"Mind telling me why?"

"You don't take rejection very well, do you?" she asked irritably. His Southern-gentleman image was slipping. "The truth is that I'm not attracted to you," she lied, almost expecting lightning to zap through the ceiling. "Now will you let go of my arms?"

"In a minute." His hand returned to her chin, tilting her head back further. "First I want to check something out."

She parted her lips to answer, only to find them covered firmly with his.

She had known it would be like this. Had known, and had tried hard to avoid it. The kiss was explosive, his touch the catalyst. Match to fuse. Gasoline to flame. Man to woman.

His tongue swept the inside of her mouth. Autumn moaned, but she could not have said whether the sound was one of pleasure or protest. She was afraid she knew, especially after he lifted his head to draw a deep breath, then lowered it again without one ounce of resistance from her.

The second kiss was just as powerful. Pressed closely together from chest to knees, Autumn was as aware of her own physical response as she was of Jeff's. Things were getting entirely out of control, she thought with some distant, still-sane portion of her brain, even as her recalcitrant hands flattened hard against his back. His image of polite gentleman had definitely altered.

It was Jeff who finally broke the kiss with obvious reluctance. He stepped back a few inches, his chest rising and falling rapidly, face slightly flushed, hands still gripping her arms through her long-sleeved knit shirt. "You want to try again?" he asked, his voice husky, his blue eyes glinting with what looked suspiciously like amusement and something else that Autumn had no need to analyze.

"Do I . . . what?" she asked, her own voice raw.

"You said you weren't attracted to me. Now we both know that's a lie, so I wondered if you wanted to try another excuse for not going out with me," he elucidated.

Autumn stared at him for a moment, her temper rising, then jerked herself out of his grasp, almost falling over the armchair behind her before catching her balance and whirling away. "You...you egotistical *male*," she hissed, snatching her cap up from the floor where it had fallen. "I said I don't want to go out with you and I meant it. I don't need an excuse."

"No, I don't suppose you do," he murmured.

Autumn glared at him through narrowed eyes, deciding that if he let loose the smile that he was obviously struggling to hold back, she'd throw something at him. How dare he laugh at her loss of temper? She took a deep breath, hid behind a facade of icy professionalism and grabbed her clipboard, holding it out to him in a curt gesture. "Sign this," she ordered, making no effort to be pleasant.

"Yes, ma'am," he murmured, lips twitching as he scrawled Dr. E. Jefferson Bradford across the bottom of the work order.

"I'll be seeing you around, Autumn," he called out to her as she climbed angrily into the cab of her pickup moments later.

"Not if I can help it," she muttered, slamming the door. She was well aware that he stood in his driveway watching her until she was completely out of his sight.

2

"Okay, Jeff, who is she?"

Jeff blinked and frowned questioningly at the woman who stood before him, determination written on her impish face as she faced him with her hands on her well-rounded hips. "Who's who?" he asked.

"The woman you've been mooning over all evening," Dr. Pamela Cochran answered flatly. In a chair across the room her husband, Bob, chuckled as he rocked his infant daughter to sleep.

Jeff glared at Bob and turned a melodramatically fierce scowl on his partner. "I have no idea what you're talking about," he told her haughtily.

Pam laughed in disbelief. "Sure you don't. Come on, Jeff, I know you. Who's the woman, and what did she do?"

"Okay, I got shot down when I asked a woman out. Twice," Jeff answered resignedly. "There, are you happy?"

Bob made a loud choking sound, startling the tiny bundle dozing in his arms. "*You* struck out?" he demanded avidly. "Will wonders never cease!"

Jeff flushed, his frown deepening as he glared at his two best friends. "Knock it off, Bob. It's not like it's the first time someone turned me down." The discussion was strangely reminiscent of his one-sided conversation two weeks earlier, after Autumn had turned him down the first time.

"Yeah? So when was the last time?" Bob inquired perceptively.

Jeff muttered the answer he'd finally come up with after asking himself the same question that other time.

"What was that? I didn't hear you," Bob insisted.

"Eleventh grade, all right?"

Bob laughed. "That's about what I thought."

Pam shook her head repressively at her husband. "And we all know that one explanation is that the man doesn't ask enough to face the usual percentage of rejection," she summed up concisely. "We're talking about the man Julian likes to call Dr. Monk."

"Most men are monks compared to Julian," Bob muttered when Jeff only snorted. "Jeff's just more concerned with quality than quantity, aren't you, buddy?"

"Since when are you two so interested in my love life?" Jeff asked them with rueful exasperation.

"Since you barely touched my special shrimp with snow peas, which happens to be your favorite Chinese dish," Pam retorted. "Only a woman could make you lose interest in shrimp with snow peas. So who is she? Do I know her?"

Jeff shook his head. "I just met her a couple of weeks ago. Her name is Autumn."

"Autumn what?"

He shrugged. "I don't know."

"Oh," Pam said slowly. "You don't know." She sat beside Jeff on her couch, staring at him with round brown eyes. "How'd you meet her?"

"She was the electrician who worked on my house when the storm knocked my service out. She came back yesterday to install an outlet in my den. I requested her specially yesterday, for all the good it did."

There was a moment of silence, and then Bob asked, "You asked your electrician out for a date?"

"Yeah. But as I said, she turned me down. Flat."

"And to think while I was trying to take care of my patients at the clinic, you were flirting with a pretty electrician," Pam complained, her eyes sparkling with the enjoyment of teasing her co-worker. "Serves you right that she turned you down."

"I acted like an idiot the first time I met her," Jeff moaned, touching his hand to his forehead. "Stuttered, stared, generally acted the fool. I wasn't much better yesterday, though I did manage not to stutter." He decided not to mention those kisses that had been almost as unexpected for him as for her. "She probably thinks I'm a not-very-bright chauvinistic jerk."

"Chauvinist? You? Hardly," Pam denied indignantly. "You're old-fashioned in some ways, but only the nicest ways," she added. "What was she . . . one of those women who gets insulted if a man simply opens a door for her?"

"Your Georgia accent is getting heavier, darling," Bob murmured, not quite successfully hiding his smile.

"I'll bet that's it. She was a Yankee, right?" Pam inquired. "Used to Northern men who walk out of elevators first and open doors only for themselves."

Jeff chuckled, his bad mood slipping away. "She's from Arkansas, Pam. No need to drag out your Rebel flag. She just isn't interested in going out with me."

"Then she has no taste," Pam proclaimed loftily. "Or she's involved with someone else. Did you ask?"

"Yes. She said there wasn't anyone else in particular."

"Then what *was* her problem?"

"Give me a break, Pam. The whole ordeal was bad enough for my ego without rehashing it. Couldn't we change the subject?"

Pam tugged thoughtfully at a curl of her frizzy brown hair. "Did I mention that we've got several fluorescent lights acting up in the clinic?" she asked finally, referring to the relatively small stucco structure the three young doctors had purchased when they'd first gone into partnership. There were advantages to owning their own building, but there were also many responsibilities—maintenance among them. "I think we need to call an electrician."

"Pamela," Jeff drawled warningly.

She widened her eyes in feigned innocence. "Well, we do," she insisted. "We can't take proper care of our patients with the lights blinking on and off."

"So call someone. But not Autumn. I don't think I could take rejection three times in a row." He sighed exaggeratedly, knowing he would make her laugh.

He was right. "Poor baby," Pam crooned when the laughter had died away. "Would a big slice of my cherry cheesecake make you feel better?"

Jeff grinned. "I'm sure it would," he said eagerly.

"Hey, I could use some cheering up myself," Bob added quickly.

"Put the baby to bed and I'll cut you a slice," Pam replied. She patted Jeff's head maternally as she stood, though she was only two years older than his thirty-three. "Don't you worry about a thing, Jeff, honey. Pam will take care of it."

"Now *that* makes me worry," Jeff answered hastily. Anytime her Georgia accent got so heavy that she called him "Jay-uff" and herself "Pay-um," he could bet that she had some kind of scheme floating around in her brilliant head. "Pamela, promise me you won't . . ." His voice faded as he followed her into the kitchen, knowing as he spoke that he was being ignored.

"DAMN THAT MAN," Autumn muttered when she realized she'd been staring at her mouth in the mirror for a good three minutes after she'd finished brushing her teeth. It had been four days since Jeff Bradford had kissed her—assaulted her, she amended vindictively—and still she had the oddest tingling sensation in her lips whenever she thought of him. Unfortunately, she thought of him much too often. Like about a thousand times a day, she added glumly, sighing as she turned off the bathroom light.

Her huge Cincinnati Reds T-shirt flapped around her bare legs as she padded across the room and climbed into her narrow white iron bed. It was barely ten o'clock, but she'd had a particularly strenuous day at work, and she was tired. She wanted nothing more than to be asleep by the time her head hit the pillow. "Good night, Babs," she told the fuzzy white miniature poodle who'd curled up beside her.

Twenty minutes had passed before Autumn finally acknowledged that she wasn't going to fall instantly asleep. She wondered wearily why she'd thought tonight would be any different from the last three. Every time she closed her eyes in the darkness, she imagined herself being held once again in the arms of a dark-haired man with the smile of an angel and the kiss of a charming devil.

It might be easier to forget him if there was even the slightest doubt that she would ever see him again, she decided. There wasn't. Dr. Jeff Bradford wouldn't disappear easily from her life now that he had unexpectedly entered it. Her luck just didn't run that way. She would see him again. And he would ask her out again. And it would be even harder to turn him down the next time. Because her lips still tingled four days after he'd kissed her. Damn.

If only she could have stayed angry with him for kissing her, for refusing to take her at her word when she'd refused to go out with him. Unfortunately, she suspected that she'd never really been angry with him in the first place but rather with herself for responding to him so dramatically.

She had to keep reminding herself why she should not go out with him. Those tingling lips were part of the reason. Never had she reacted to any man's kiss in quite that manner. It wouldn't take many of those kisses to have her dragging him off to bed. And conservative, reluctantly conventional woman that she was in some ways, she'd end up wanting more than sex from him. Before she knew it, she'd be sorting his socks and dyeing his underwear pink with her haphazard laundry habits. She could say goodbye to blissful independence, unconcernedly irregular hours, gourmet frozen dinners. Hello to slow, deadly suffocation. She'd been there before.

Steven had been blond, rugged and attentive. His slow smiles and practiced caresses had awakened Autumn's teenage body to its first taste of desire. The fiery-tempered tomboy had changed into a passionate young woman madly infatuated for the first time. Despite the budding ideas of women's liberation gained from her avid reading about "life in the outside world," her small-town Arkansas Baptist upbringing had led her to consider it only fitting that back-seat experimentation should lead to an engagement ring given the night she graduated from high school.

Steven had been attending agricultural college at Arkansas State University, and Autumn had been content to do office work for a small electrical service in her hometown of Rose Bud while waiting for Steven to graduate. Or at least she had tried to be content, despite the ever-increasing surges of pure panic that assailed her whenever she allowed herself to contemplate a future in Rose Bud with two or three kids and a husband whose destiny was to take over the family farm and raise soybeans and grain. She kept reading—*Cosmopolitan*, *Ms.*, other magazines targeted at young, single career women—kept fantasizing about doing something on her own, finding out what it might be like to build a life for herself. And kept trying to pretend she was happy.

Autumn wasn't sure when the occasional bouts of panic had turned to outright rebellion. She remembered watching with growing envy as the electricians she worked for went off on jobs, patting her on the head and calling her "honey" as they passed her on their way out. She remembered the resentment that had begun to build when Steven had casually asked her to bring him a beer or fix him a plate at dinner, his attempts to tame her temper and natural independence. She remembered how hard it had been each morning to slide on that miniature diamond ring that felt heavier all the time. And she remembered the desperation she'd felt when both of her sisters had moved out, Spring to college in Memphis, Summer to college in Little Rock, leaving Autumn at home in Rose Bud feeling as if she'd never be able to escape.

She hadn't eased gracefully out of the engagement. She hadn't even been conscious of making the decision to end it. One summer evening just before her twentieth birthday, she'd attended a family gathering at Steven's home. The evening had been intolerable, rampant with Southern farmer sexism and probing questions about Steven and Autumn's plans for the future. Autumn had prepared Steven's plate for him—just as all the other women had done for their men—and later had helped clean the kitchen while Steven had joined the other males in front of the television. The second time Steven had called for a beer, Autumn had obediently carried it to him. And then kept walking, straight out the front door and out of sexy Steven's life for good. Two months later she'd been living in Little Rock, attending electrician's classes one night a week at a vo-tech school while working as an apprentice during the day.

It had been five years since she'd broken up with Steven. Since that time she'd earned her journeyman's license and had developed her independence to an art. She liked living in Florida, enjoyed working for Brothers Electrical while putting in the two years required between obtaining her journeyman's license and taking the test that would earn her master's license. Someday she would like to start her own electrical contracting company. Sure she was lonely sometimes, but not enough to jeopardize the life she'd built for herself.

She tried to tell herself that she was making too big an issue out of two brief meetings with an admittedly attractive man. She argued with herself that she could even go out with the guy without destroying her treasured self-sufficiency. After all, she barely knew him.

Running from him in blind panic at this point was nothing more than hysterical overreaction. She went out with other guys, didn't she? She'd maintained a healthy, normal social life during the past five years, though she'd never really developed a taste for casual sex. She was being an idiot to lie awake worrying about going out with a man she had only just met, may never hear from again. If she had any sense, she'd put him completely out of her mind, decide what to do when— or *if* he asked her out again.

And yet her lips still tingled.

She groaned and pulled the sheets over her head, completely covering both herself and her disgruntled dog.

AUTUMN WORE a rueful smile as she pushed open the sparkling glass door of the Tampa Pediatrics Clinic and stepped into the colorfully decorated lobby. The waiting area was crowded with mothers and children, even though it was the day after Thanksgiving—perhaps because of it, she thought whimsically, wondering how many of the children had overdosed on turkey and pumpkin pie. She hadn't been at all surprised to see Dr. E. Jefferson Bradford's name printed in gold letters on the outside of the building, along with the names of two other doctors. But then, she'd been expecting to see his name since she'd been informed that the customer had specifically requested her services for this job. Dodging an active toddler on her way to the reception desk, Autumn told herself that she admired Jeff's persistence almost as much as his nice bod.

She still had not come to a conclusion about what to do when he asked her out this time. Part of her wanted to accept, the same part of her that had been so relieved that he had not given up on her, though it had been three weeks and one day since she'd heard from him. The same part that tried to tell her that she was being ridiculous to keep turning him down simply because she was afraid of her powerful attraction to him. Another part of her was terrified of that same attraction.

The pretty brunette receptionist nodded when Autumn gave her name and company. "Oh, yes, Dr. Cochran said she wanted to see you when you arrived. She's just finishing up with a patient, so you can go into her office and she'll be right with you." She gave Autumn directions to the office, then turned to greet a woman holding a feverish-looking child in her arms.

Autumn frowned a little as she walked down the hallway, pausing at an open door stenciled with the name Dr. Pamela Cochran. She'd expected to be taken directly to Jeff. Who was Pamela Cochran?

The office was cluttered in a rather organized way. The wall held diplomas and certificates, bookshelves overflowed with technical-looking volumes and file folders were piled haphazardly on the desk. A gold frame held a photograph of a smiling, dimpled baby. One of the fluorescent lights above the desk was out.

"Oh, hello," came a melodic, very Southern voice from the doorway. "You must be Autumn."

Autumn turned her head as a pleasantly plain woman with dancing brown eyes and frizzy brown hair entered the office. The woman—Dr. Cochran, Autumn assumed from the white lab coat worn over a blue cotton dress, a stethoscope dangling from a deep side pocket—was looking back at Autumn with a broad smile. And something else. Speculation? Curiosity? Autumn returned the smile automatically, wondering if Jeff had said anything to this woman about his two previous encounters with Autumn. "Yes, I'm Autumn Reed. You're Dr. Cochran?"

"Sure am," Dr. Cochran replied cheerfully. "I hear you're a marvelous electrician—"

Autumn hid a grin at the number of syllables the woman managed to work into those two words. And she'd thought *her* Southern accent was heavy!

"So I asked for you specifically when I called your company. I wasn't sure you'd be working on the day after a holiday."

Autumn blinked. Dr. Cochran had called her? "Yes, I'm taking extra time at Christmas, so I chose to work today," she explained, speaking without really thinking because she was still trying to decide why Jeff had not called himself.

"Lucky for us," the doctor commented. "We're having some trouble with some of our lights. Some of them are out, like the one above my desk, and then there are a couple that are blinking and making the most irritating buzzing noise." She reeled off the entire sentence without once pronouncing a *G*.

Autumn had to smile at the woman then. "The ballasts need changing," she explained, instinctively liking Dr. Pamela Cochran. "It won't take long. I'll try to stay out of the way while I work, unless you'd rather I'd take care of it after the clinic closes for the day."

"No, that's okay," the other woman assured her. "I'll have Kelly, one of our assistants, show you around. She'll let you know which examining rooms are being used. We'll all work around each other." She gave Autumn a friendly, conspiratorial wink. "That way the clinic won't have to pay time and a half for your services."

"Very practical," Autumn murmured. She definitely liked Dr. Cochran.

"Pam, I need you in room three. I've got a patient who's going to need surgery and—Autumn!" Jeff stopped abruptly halfway through the doorway, staring at the young woman in the plaid cotton blouse and khaki pants, the ever-present baseball cap tugged over her auburn braid.

He hadn't known she was coming. He had given up on her after all. Autumn swallowed her disappointment and tried to look nonchalant, though her heart was beating wildly in her chest. Lord, he looked good in his white coat, which he wore over a pearl-gray shirt with a maroon tie and charcoal slacks. She'd only seen him in casual clothes before. Now, with his crisp black hair neatly combed and his beautiful biceps hidden beneath the uniform of his profession, he looked... different. Dr. E. Jefferson Bradford. Autumn suddenly felt self-conscious, awkward.

And then he smiled, his delectable mouth parting to show his even white teeth and deeply slashed dimples, his blue eyes crinkling a little at the corners, and he was the Jeff Bradford she'd met at his house. Ridiculously young looking, sinfully handsome, even a bit shy. She smiled back. "Hi, Jeff."

"Here to work on the lights?" he asked, and even his voice had changed. It had been harried, brisk, when he'd spoken to Pam as he'd entered; now it was husky, slightly intimate.

Cursing her light complexion, Autumn felt the color staining her cheeks. "Yes."

"I'm afraid I won't be able to help you this time," he told her with a grin. "I'm rather busy."

"I'll manage," she answered dryly.

"I'm sure you will," he returned softly. He glanced back at Pam, who was watching them with unconcealed, avid interest. "Got time for a consultation?" he asked her, trying to sound stern.

"Of course," Pam replied, unintimidated.

"Come on, then." He glanced back at Autumn. "Don't leave without saying goodbye," he said, the words phrased like an order but sounding like a request. Particularly when he added, "Please."

She nodded. He was giving her warning, she thought desperately. He was going to ask her out again. Why couldn't she make a decision about whether or not to accept?

With Kelly as her helper, Autumn went about her job. Though she stayed discreetly out of his way, Autumn was able to observe Jeff at work, struck again by the change in him when he assumed the mien of physician. He was great with children, naturally. Gentle, patient, indulgent. He should have children of his own, she thought fleetingly, then deliberately blanked her mind as she tried to concentrate on her work.

When she'd finished and had carried her tools and ladder out to the truck, Autumn hesitated before seeking Jeff. As it turned out, it wasn't necessary. He found her. "All done?" he inquired.

She nodded, fidgeting with her clipboard as she waited for him to issue the invitation she expected. She was *not* nervous, she told herself firmly. After all, even if she accepted, it would only be a dinner date. Pleasant, unthreatening, completely innocuous. She surreptitiously wiped her damp palms on the legs of her khaki pants, looking up at Jeff through her lashes.

Jeff had been watching her closely, suppressing an urge to chuckle when he realized that she was actually showing signs of agitation. He hadn't thought it possible that there was any shyness at all within this supremely self-confident young feminist. Suddenly all trace of his own uncertainty disappeared. Would she be shy if she weren't attracted to him at least a little? he asked himself hopefully.

She was so obviously expecting him to ask her out again. He had intended to do just that. He wondered what her answer would be this time. And then he wondered what her reaction would be when he didn't ask. He had just changed his strategy.

"Did you have a nice Thanksgiving?" he asked, pleased when she gave a little start at the sound of his voice. She *was* nervous.

Autumn nodded. "Yes, thank you." She and Babs had indulged in a frozen turkey breast and steamed fresh vegetables while watching a football game together on television. She had also talked by telephone to her parents and to her two married sisters, one of whom lived in California, the other in Arkansas. It *had* been a nice day, she told herself, ignoring the slight sense of loneliness that remained.

"So did I. Spent the day with my folks in Sarasota. Actually, though, I wanted to talk to you about something else."

Here it comes. Autumn tried to make a snap decision, failing miserably. "What?"

"I'm considering installing new outdoor lighting, particularly around the pool. What would you recommend?"

Outdoor lighting? Was he serious? "I would have to see it before I could make a recommendation," she answered slowly. "I haven't seen your pool."

He nodded. "Of course. I'll call your company and try to schedule time with you next Thursday, if you're not already booked up."

"Fine." She waited, but he said nothing more. He seemed to be waiting for her to say something. But what? "I, um, I guess I'll see you later, then."

"I'll walk you out."

Autumn carefully avoided looking at him as they walked together down the long, bright hallway. If his purpose was to confuse her, he had certainly done it. At the door she glanced up at him to find him looking back at her with a broad smile. "Goodbye, Autumn."

"Bye, Jeff." She stepped through the door he was holding for her, then paused when he said her name.

"Autumn?"

"Yes?"

"This could go on a long time. Until I run out of electrical ideas. Or money," he added thoughtfully. Before she could answer, he had closed the door quietly in her face.

She stared blankly at that door for a long moment, then started to laugh. He was challenging her! He had just subtly let her know that he was going to keep calling her until she agreed to go out with him. He hadn't given up on her!

Oh, Lord, she shouldn't be feeling this giddy sense of relief. She shouldn't be fighting the urge to dance back to the truck or to burst into song.

"Autumn, you are such a fool," she groaned, tugging down the bill of her cap as she settled behind the wheel of the truck.

"THIS IS RIDICULOUS," Autumn muttered some five hours later, after she'd changed the channel on the television set for the fourth time in a half hour. Nothing on the small screen interested her, and neither did the thick mystery novel she'd purchased only the day before. She was trying not to think about Jeff Bradford, but her progress so far was lousy.

With a gusty sigh she snapped off the television and roamed into the kitchen of her duplex apartment, remembering that she hadn't yet gotten around to eating dinner. She burrowed in the cabinets and refrigerator, but nothing looked overly appealing. She finally settled on a sandwich made from the remains of the frozen turkey breast and a handful of frosted animal cookies.

Having finished the sandwich without enthusiasm, she carried the cookies into the modern burgundy-and-dark-green living room, where she dropped onto the boldly flowered chintz sofa and finally allowed herself to think about Jeff.

She curled her bare feet under her and munched on a pink lion, deep in thought until a gentle whine turned her attention to the floor beside her. "Sorry, Babs, did you want a cookie?" she asked the poodle, who was looking hopefully up at her. The dog yipped a reply.

"Elephant or rhinoceros?" Autumn inquired.

Babs yipped again.

"Elephant it is." Autumn tossed the cookie to the dog, smiling a little as Babs caught it deftly and began to eat with delicate nibbles.

Her gaze on her pet's amusing greed, Autumn finally gave in to the need to think seriously about the subject preying so heavily on her mind. E. Jefferson Bradford. She'd never reacted to any man this way. He had only to look at her, much less give her one of those smiles of his, to turn her to Jell-O, a new experience for Autumn Reed.

Her cookie eaten, Babs hopped into Autumn's lap and, standing on her hind legs, planted a wet kiss on Autumn's chin. Autumn hugged the squirming little body and chuckled. "So what do you think I should do about him, Babs?" she asked whimsically.

Babs wiggled and made a playful growling sound low in her throat.

"Go out with him, huh? Sounds easy enough, but I have a feeling that I'd be getting into something I don't know how to handle. For one thing, what could we talk about?"

Autumn cocked an eyebrow at the dog. "That's all very well for you to say," she muttered as if Babs had actually made a suggestion. "But if we spend an evening *not* talking, I'll be in even worse trouble."

The dog barked sharply. Autumn sighed. "He's turning me into a basket case. I'm actually sitting here having a conversation with a dog."

Babs looked hurt.

"Oh, sorry, Babs. I didn't mean anything personal."

Babs jumped down to the floor, stopping by the telephone table to scratch her ear on her way to the doggie door in the kitchen that gave her access to the small, fenced backyard of Autumn's half of the duplex. Taking that as a hint, Autumn sighed and walked slowly to the telephone. "You're right, Babs. I can't go on like this. It's time to take action."

Jeff's number was listed in the telephone book. Autumn hung up twice before she could make herself dial it. It wasn't that she'd never called a man for a date, but she had never called Dr. E. Jefferson Bradford. What was it about him that was so different from other men?

Finally she dialed the number and waited for the ring. She told herself that he probably wasn't home. After all, it *was* Friday night. And if he was out, fine. It wasn't meant to be.

"Hello?"

Well, hell, he was home. "Um, Jeff?"

"Autumn?"

She supposed she should be flattered that he immediately recognized her voice. "Yes. I hope I'm not disturbing you." *Dumb thing to say*, she told herself immediately. *He'll think I'm asking if he's alone.* She continued quickly. "I was just wondering . . . do you really want new lighting outside your house?"

3

JEFF PAUSED FOR A MOMENT, then chuckled. "Well, I have to admit it was a spur-of-the-moment suggestion on my part, but I suppose I could think of something else for you to do if you'd rather."

"Look, why don't we just forget the games," Autumn told him impatiently. "We both know you're only doing the lights so you can ask me out again, right?"

"I have no intention of asking you out again," Jeff replied decisively.

She narrowed her eyes, fingers tightening on the dark red plastic receiver. "You don't?" she asked, her disbelief obvious in her voice.

"No, ma'am. A man can only take so much rejection," he drawled.

Oh, Lord. First a Southern gentleman, now an Old West cowhand. "Are you doing anything tomorrow night?" she asked bluntly.

"That depends. Why are you asking?"

She thought seriously about slamming the phone down in his ear but controlled herself. "Would you like to go out to dinner with me? Maybe we could go dancing or something afterward."

"Gee, I don't know. This is so sudden."

Autumn tried very hard not to be amused. "Dammit, Jeff, yes or no?"

He laughed, the sound warming her even through the telephone line. "I really need to study your technique for asking for a date," he told her. "Such charm. Such tact."

"Jeff . . ." Her voice informed him quite clearly that he was about to find himself talking to a dial tone.

"Okay, you've talked me into it. What time are you picking me up?"

"How's seven grab you?"

"Seven grabs me just fine. Thanks for asking."

Autumn did hang up then, and none too gently.

"I hope you're happy," she told Babs, glaring at the innocent-looking animal who'd just come back into the room, happily wagging her tail as she looked up at Autumn. "I just made a first-class fool out of myself. Why do I let him do that to me?"

Babs gave a poodle equivalent of a shrug and settled herself into a lazy curl on the carpet, signifying her desire for a nap. Autumn sighed and picked up her book again. The sad part was, she decided as she unenthusiastically opened it, that she really had wanted to ask Jeff if he was alone.

JEFF LAUGHED when the phone went abruptly dead. Autumn Reed was really something, he mused as he replaced his own receiver, more gently than she had. Although he'd chewed Pam out but good earlier for interfering, he was actually glad that she'd taken the initiative to call Autumn to the clinic. If she hadn't, Jeff would have eventually. Besides, if Pam hadn't told him, he still wouldn't know Autumn's last name.

He was doubly glad now that he hadn't asked Autumn out at the clinic. By doing the unexpected and leaving it up to her, he had stumbled upon exactly the right strategy for the stubborn, defiant woman. He had to pause for a moment to ask himself exactly what it was about her that attracted him so strongly, but the answer wasn't hard to come by. He was enthralled with her. He'd never met anyone quite like her.

She tried so hard to be tough, invulnerable. She probably even believed she succeeded. But Jeff had seen her wet her lips in an unconscious gesture of nerves, had felt her tremble in his arms, had seen the color stain her cheeks when she was embarrassed. She wasn't so tough. She'd been nervous during that phone call, despite her snippy manner. He wondered who had hurt her so badly that she'd felt it necessary to erect such a brittle shell around her inner softness.

He'd dated a few women who had really been hard, who had completely eliminated that inner softness. Autumn wasn't one of them, thank God, no matter how she might try to appear to be. Those wide green eyes of hers gave her away. She was a witch, a sorceress, but there was vulnerability behind her skillful spells. Jeff intended to find that vulnerability.

Though she wouldn't appreciate it one bit, something about her brought out the protective instincts within him. He was caught in her spell—so well trapped that he had no desire to free himself. Perhaps this was only infatuation that he felt for her, nothing more than fascinated desire, but it was a powerful emotion. Like nothing he'd ever felt before. How could he turn away without finding out exactly what it was that possessed him?

When he pursued, she ran.

It seemed that he was going to have to be the pursued.

Jeff grinned and tugged his gray sweatshirt over his head, moving toward the bedroom. The sooner he went to bed, the sooner the next day would come. And the sooner he would be with Autumn again.

GRINDING A CURSE OUT between clenched teeth, Autumn jerked the striped dress over her head and threw it on her bed, where it landed in a slither of color on top of a pile of similarly discarded garments. "Stupid, stupid, stupid!" she wailed, shoving her hands through her auburn mane as she stared into her closet.

She should call and cancel, she decided. She could tell Jeff she was sick. Or in jail. She wouldn't tell him the truth—that just over an hour before their date, she'd regressed to adolescence. She had somehow been transformed from a modern, competent woman to a silly, dithering teenager, and damned if she could figure out a way to change back. She didn't know what to wear, she wasn't sure what to say or do when she saw him, she was even starting to worry about the good-night kiss. "Maybe it's a regressive brain disease," she mused aloud, causing Babs to look at her with interest. It just had to be biological. Surely a simple Saturday-night dinner date wouldn't do this to her!

Her doorbell distracted her, and she frowned as she wrapped herself in a terry robe. She wasn't expecting anyone. She decided it must be her neighbor, Emily, with whom she had become friends during the three months that Emily and her son, Ryan, had occupied the other half of the large duplex. Crossing her living room, she glanced perfunctorily out the peephole and groaned. "What are you doing here, Webb?" she asked as she opened the door.

"Thanks, Autumn, I'd love to come in." Webb Brothers grinned lazily at her as he strolled past her, hands in the pockets of his jeans. Tall, lanky, sandy-haired Webb was the son of Autumn's boss, Floyd Brothers, owner of Brothers Electrical Company. It had been Webb who'd convinced his skeptical, traditional father to give a woman electrician—Autumn—a chance to prove herself. Webb had been her champion, her co-worker and her friend ever since. He also took great pleasure in teasing her, and it was that particular trait that had her eyeing him warily now. She was determined to hide her current emotional state from his all-too-perceptive eyes. He'd never let her live it down.

"So, my love, you want to take in a movie tonight?" he asked, tilting his light brown head in a stance he'd carefully copied from Robert Redford because someone had once told him he resembled the attractive actor. Autumn thought he looked a bit like the young Redford, but she would never tell him so. Webb was in no need of ego strokes.

"I'm not your love, and I can't go to a movie with you tonight. I have a date." In barely an hour. And she still didn't know what she was going to wear. Swallowing a moan, she narrowed her green eyes at him. "What are you doing free on a Saturday night, anyway? Don't tell me that Webb Brothers couldn't get a date!"

He grimaced at her and dropped into a burgundy-and-dark-green striped armchair. "Maybe I just wanted to do something with you."

"If you'd wanted to do something with me, you'd have mentioned it at work yesterday," she pointed out, perching on the edge of the sofa and trying to hide her impatience to get back to her dressing trauma.

Webb scooped an eager Babs into his arms and began to scratch behind her long fluffy ears, apparently in no hurry to leave. "Okay, so my date canceled out," he admitted. "She was called out of town on a business crisis. I thought since I was free, I'd see what you were doing."

"Ever heard of the telephone, Brothers?"

He shrugged good-naturedly. "This is more fun. I can watch you dress." He gave her a suggestive leer, part of the teasing flirting that had developed between them over their year-long friendship.

"Wrong."

"Then I'll wait and check out your date when he gets here."

"Wrong again. I'm picking him up."

"Well, hell, Reed. You take all the fun out of everything."

"Sorry." She wasn't, of course, and her smile told him so.

"So who are you going out with tonight? Terry? Rick? Dwayne?" he asked, naming her three most common escorts, men she liked and whose company she enjoyed, though her relationship with each of them was light and platonic.

"None of the above."

"Oh?" Autumn fancied that Webb's ears perked up with interest, as Babs's did when she heard an unusual noise. "Someone new?"

"Yeah."

"Do I know him?"

"I doubt it."

Webb sighed loudly. "This is like pulling teeth. What's his name, Autumn?"

"His name's Jeff Bradford," Autumn returned in resignation, even the sound of Jeff's name making her shiver. Lord, she was still doing it!

"Jeff Bradford, the doctor?" Webb asked with a lifted eyebrow.

Oh, no, not a friend of Webb's, Autumn thought with a mental groan. "Yes. Do you know him?"

"Yeah, I've known him a few years. We belong to the same health club, and we're in the same Jaycees chapter, though he's not quite as active in it as I am. His work keeps him too busy."

She shouldn't be surprised that Webb knew Jeff. Tampa wasn't that large a city, and Webb got around. Still, Autumn wished that he and Jeff were total strangers. If she was going to make a fool of herself over Jeff Bradford—and she pessimistically suspected that she was—she preferred to do it in total privacy. She had toyed with the idea of throwing herself into a crazy affair with the attractive young doctor until she'd worked out her foolish infatuation with him, at which time she would cheerfully tell him goodbye and return to her sane, carefully controlled life, with no one the wiser but her and Jeff. Now she had an audience. The smartest thing to do was to keep Webb from finding out the strange effect that Dr. Jeff Bradford had had on her from the moment she'd met him.

"So how'd you meet Jeff, anyway?" Webb asked curiously.

Autumn explained briefly, then tried to change the subject by adding, "I'll be glad when you and the rest of the crew finish up that shopping mall remodel. I'm getting all the small, one-person jobs these days."

Her diversion seemed to work. "That reminds me," Webb commented, setting Babs on the floor, "you'll be working with us for the next couple of weeks. Chuck's going to take over the stuff you've been doing."

"How come?"

Webb shrugged and made a face. "He can't seem to get along with the property manager who's supervising the remodel. The guy's a jerk, but Chuck needs to learn when to keep his mouth shut. Okay with you?"

"Sure. Uh, Webb, I really need to start getting ready for my date now," she hinted broadly, hating to bring up the subject again but anxious to get dressed—if she could ever decide what she was going to wear.

"Don't mind me. I think I'll have a beer." Webb pushed himself out of the chair and headed for the kitchen.

Autumn sighed. "Just make yourself at home," she muttered.

He threw her a grin over his shoulder. "I'll do that."

Shaking her head in exasperation, she walked into her bedroom. She hadn't closed the door yet when Webb appeared behind her. "I forgot to ask," he said, "do you want one, too?"

"No, thanks," she answered quickly, turning to hustle him out of the room.

Too late. He was standing in exaggerated open-mouthed astonishment, staring at the pile of clothing strewn across her bed. "If I didn't know better, I would swear this is my sister's room prior to a date with one of her college jocks," he marveled. He looked at Autumn with a questioning frown. "Tell me that you haven't been trying on everything in your wardrobe for the past half hour."

She exhaled slowly. "So I'm having a little trouble deciding what to wear," she admitted belligerently. "What of it?"

Webb leaned back against the doorjamb and laughed. Heartily. "This," he said when he could speak, "from the woman who wore a baseball cap and sweat-

shirt to a wedding shower? Who considers herself really
dressed up if her jeans have a name on the back
pocket?"

Autumn glared at him. "Okay, so I'm not on the best-
dressed list. Most of the time I wear jeans and shirts because I work at a blue-collar job and I like to be comfortable. I think women who spend a fortune on
clothing and follow every fleeting dictate of fashion are
in bad need of something productive to do. But I still
want to look halfway decent on a date, and I don't see
anything to laugh about!"

Webb shook his brownish-blond head in amusement. "I'm not laughing because you want to look nice.
To me, you always look nice. You dress casually, but
you've got a style of your own. I was laughing because
you look so harried and nervous. That's not like you,
Autumn. Don't tell me that you've fallen for Jeff Bradford."

"Don't be ridiculous! I hardly know him."

"Mmm. So how come you're blushing?"

"I am *not* blushing!" She threw her hands up to cover
cheeks that felt suspiciously hot. "Oh, hell, I *am*
blushing."

Webb laughed again. "Kind of like the guy, huh?"

She sighed. "Yeah, I like him. But," she added
quickly, "that doesn't mean there's any big romance
developing between us or anything like that."

"Of course not," Webb agreed gravely. "I know your
policy about serious relationships—if there's the
slightest fragrance of orange blossoms or hint of wedding bells in the air, you head for the hills. Figuratively
speaking, of course."

"Isn't that very similar to your own policy?" Autumn inquired crossly, knowing that Webb was every bit as antimarriage as she.

"Of course it is. That's why you and I are such good friends. And why I've never tried to put the moves on you."

She eyed him suspiciously. "The reason you've never tried to 'put the moves' on me is because I'm not your type. We've always been just friends."

He shook his head, brown eyes dancing teasingly at her. "The reason I've kept us 'just friends' is that you're marriage bait if I've ever seen it. You can talk all you want to about staying footloose and single, but when you fall in love, you'll be heading down that aisle just like your two sisters did during the past year. I was just making sure that I wasn't the guy waiting at the altar for you, lovely though you are."

"You're an arrogant, conceited creep, Brothers. I wouldn't have seriously dated you if you'd asked," she told him flatly, irritated at his accusation. "*You're* the one who's marriage bait!"

He looked startled. "You're crazy!"

"Yeah? I don't think you'd deny it so furiously if you didn't think you were susceptible to the weakness. Every time you start to get close to a woman, you turn pale and run. How come, huh?"

"I *like* being single," her thirty-one-year-old friend answered earnestly. "I like not answering to anyone, not worrying about mortgages and bills, not saving for college funds or second honeymoons. I like going out with a redhead one night, a blonde the next and a brunette the night after that."

"You can talk all you want about staying footloose and single, but when you fall in love, you'll be heading

down that aisle just like your brother did last month,"
Autumn paraphrased primly, tossing her head so that
her hair flew out, then settled in a thick, cinnamon
curtain around her shoulders. "Now would you get out
of here?" she demanded before he could voice the argument that she could see on his face. "I have to get
dressed and I still don't know what to wear."

"Where are you going?"

"Dinner and dancing."

"Wear that gold thing."

Autumn looked doubtful. "You think so?"

"Trust me. I know so."

The gold thing. Autumn chewed on her lower lip,
wondering if that choice would be at all wise. She shot
a suspicious look at Webb, who was grinning from ear
to ear. She was just about to speak when the doorbell
rang again.

"What is this tonight...the gathering place for all of
Tampa?" she asked her bedroom wall, tossing up her
hands at this new interruption. "I don't even have my
makeup on!"

"Autumn, I'm sorry to bother you, but do you have
any milk? Can you believe I've run out?" Emily Hinson, Autumn's neighbor, stood on the doorstep, her
fifteen-month-old son, Ryan, on her hip holding his favorite stuffed dog. Divorced since shortly after Ryan's
birth, twenty-three-year-old Emily was Autumn's opposite in almost every way. She was delicate in appearance, if not in actuality, petite and blond with
enormous china-blue eyes. She enjoyed her work as a
secretary, loved cooking and needlework and all other
things domestic, and made it no secret that she would
like to be married again despite the failure of her first
marriage. And yet the two women had become friends

from almost the moment they'd met outside their duplex when Emily had moved in.

"There's milk in the refrigerator. Help yourself, I'm dressing for a date," Autumn told her, patting Ryan's chubby cheek as he grinned wetly at her.

Emily started in, then paused at the sight of Webb. "Oh, I'm sorry. I didn't know your date was already here."

"Oh, that's not my date. That's just Webb." Autumn was already halfway through the door to her bedroom. "Introduce yourself, Webb. I *have* to get ready!"

Thirty minutes later she took a deep breath and checked her appearance in the mirror. Even she could admit that she looked good. She wondered what Jeff would think.

Webb, Emily and Ryan looked up and blinked when Autumn came out of her bedroom to join them in the living room. Autumn hadn't realized that Emily was still there. It appeared that Emily and Webb had been talking easily for the past half hour while Autumn had dressed, Ryan playing with his toy on the carpet at their feet. "Autumn, you look beautiful!" Emily breathed, staring at the metamorphosis.

Webb shook his sandy head and grinned. "I told you the gold thing would be the right choice," he said smugly.

Autumn grimaced. "I hope it's not too much."

"It's not too much. Believe me," Webb answered solemnly, turning a smile to Emily. "What do you think, Emily?"

"I think it's gorgeous. And I truly wish it were my size so I could borrow it for a date sometime," Emily added with a light laugh. "Not that it would do for me what it does for Autumn."

Webb looked startled. "A date? Oh, you mean with your husband."

"Oh, I'm not married," Emily corrected him, looking a bit surprised that he didn't already know. "I've been divorced for a year."

Webb swallowed, looked at her again, then all but leaped to his feet. "Well, I have to go," he announced a bit too loudly. "Have a good time on your date, Autumn. Tell Bradford I said hello. Nice to meet you, Emily. Bye, Ryan." And then he was gone.

Emily frowned at the door that had closed behind him, then turned her bewildered gaze to Autumn. "Was it something I said?"

Autumn only laughed.

JEFF SHRUGGED into the jacket of his charcoal-gray pinstriped suit, adjusted his yellow silk tie and glanced at the thin gold watch on his wrist. Five minutes until seven. Five minutes until he saw Autumn. He took a deep breath, trying to calm his nervous stomach. Lord, he hadn't been so nervous before a date since...since...well, he'd never been this nervous before a date.

She was so skittish. All his instincts told him that one wrong move, one wrong word, on his part, would cause her to take flight, right out of his life. He wondered again who had hurt her, what she was afraid of and whether he would have a chance to explore his budding feelings for her without driving her away. He wasn't interested in an affair, had never been interested in empty affairs. He wanted a future, a relationship, something meaningful and enriching and nurturing. He wanted what Pam and Bob had. He'd always suspected that when he met the right woman, he would know immediately. The moment Autumn Reed had taken off her sunglasses and looked at him with those bewitching green eyes, he'd known.

Now if only he could convince her to give them a chance.

He hoped he hadn't overdressed. He'd wanted to look nice, but then Autumn seemed to be the casual type. Of course, he'd only seen her on the job so far. But then again, he thought with his one-sided smile, if she looked any more beautiful than she had the last three times he'd seen her, he might not be able to control himself.

His doorbell chimed. Jeff's heart jerked convulsively, and he swallowed, rather stunned by his own reactions. He looked in wonder at his hands. His palms were damp! Shaking his head in astonishment, he went to answer his door.

He had to make a conscious effort to keep his jaw from dropping at the vision on his doorstep.

She was the most exquisite thing he'd ever seen. Soft auburn curls glowing red in the evening sun, tumbling around her shoulders and begging for his hands. Artfully applied makeup enhancing emerald eyes and glistening lips. And that dress.

He gulped. God, that dress. Shaped like an inverted triangle with padded shoulders and bat-wing sleeves, it clung lovingly to her full breasts, then hugged the feminine curves of her hips and thighs to fall to the middle of her knees. It was made of some slinky material that looked gold at one moment, black at the next. He blinked to clear his eyes, only then realizing that the fabric was black shot with thousands of glittering gold threads.

She was beautiful, sexy, tempting. And looking at him in a defiant manner that dared him to say a word, much less follow his immediate impulse to reach out and grab her. "Would you..." He had to stop to clear his throat. "Would you like to come in for a drink?"

Was that relief he saw cross her face? Had she been so anxious about his reaction to her transformation from work clothes to evening clothes? She had good reason to be. He shoved his hands into the pockets of his suit pants, fighting all kinds of primitive urges that were as surprising to him as they would have been to her, had he followed through on them.

And then she walked past him, and he had to swallow a moan. The dress had no back. From the button at the top of her shoulders to the top of the skirt, there was nothing but silky bare skin and the delicate ridges of her spine. The skirt was split in the center to allow glimpses of the backs of her knees as she walked.

He turned his eyes heavenward as he closed the front door. "This is some kind of test, right?" he murmured beneath his breath. He remembered all his earlier resolutions about watching his step with her, being careful not to frighten her off, and he felt himself on the verge of hysterical laughter. How could he possibly have known that she would show up looking like...like *this*?

"Did you say something?" Autumn asked curiously, turning to look at him.

"Just praying," he answered, then before she could comment, "What would you like to drink?"

She looked at him rather oddly, then moistened her lower lip with the tip of her tongue. Jeff closed his eyes for a moment. This was *definitely* a test.

"I don't believe I want anything, thanks," Autumn was saying when he opened his eyes again.

Come to think of it, neither did he. The one thing he did *not* need just now was anything that might possibly weaken his control. Autumn was intoxicating enough. "Then I suppose we're ready to go."

She nodded, twisting her hands in front of her. "Yes, I'm ready."

This might turn out to be a very long evening, Jeff thought wryly as he held the door for her to pass him. Without really thinking about it, he started to place a hand on her back, then jerked the hand away when he encountered bare flesh. A *very* long evening.

Resigning himself to always acting like a thick-skulled, not-really-bright clod in this woman's presence, he followed her to her sporty black Fiero, knowing better than to offer to drive—or to open her door for her.

4

AUTUMN CAREFULLY AVOIDED Jeff's eyes as she started her car, though she was all too conscious of him within the confines of her small Fiero. Her hand was only inches from his thigh when she reached out to shift into reverse. Unable to resist, she glanced at that thigh, so solid and powerful beneath the fabric of his gray suit, and then her gaze drifted upward to his lap. She gulped and turned her eyes firmly forward, away from the tempting territory of his masculinity.

It was going to be a long evening. She'd regretted her choice of clothing ever since he'd opened the door and immediately looked like a man who'd been kicked in the gut by the Karate Kid. She'd worn the dress only once before, to a party she'd attended with Webb. After a night of being pawed by strangers, she'd decided never to wear it again. So why had she let Webb talk her into it tonight? she asked herself in disgust.

Trust me, he'd said. She should have known right then to choose something else. Though some perverse feminine part of her was secretly pleased by Jeff's unspoken appreciation, a more rational part of her was cautious of the sparks that were so obviously flying between them. It had never been like this for her before. Never.

The silence in the car was growing deafening. She glanced sideways at Jeff, finding him watching her with a faint, enigmatic smile, as if he were waiting for her to say something. She was fully aware that she'd barely spoken to him since she'd picked him up, but she didn't know what to say. What she really wanted to do was stop, turn in her seat and just stare at him for about an hour. No man should be that good-looking. It simply wasn't fair. It was nature's way of keeping liberated women on their toes, she decided. Give a guy thick black hair, deep blue eyes and a smile that could melt the gold tips on the toes of her black shoes and watch Autumn turn to oatmeal.

When the silence began to sizzle with tension, she reached out almost desperately and pushed a cassette into the player on the dash, not even noticing what she'd chosen. She smiled wryly when the music swelled out at the high level she generally preferred. Simple Minds. Appropriate choice of bands.

She didn't know why she was behaving this way, why she was on the defensive. She only knew that Jeff Bradford was the most dangerous man she'd ever met and that she would have to stay on the defensive to survive him with heart and pride intact.

She should have worn a different dress.

Jeff tolerated the loud music for a time, then reached out and firmly turned down the volume. Autumn threw him a startled look. "You don't like rock music?" she demanded as if he'd be confessing to all sorts of terrible crimes if he did not.

"I like rock music," he answered. "I like Simple Minds," he added to point out that he had recognized the group. "But I also like to converse with my date."

"Oh."

He fought a grin without much success. She was cute when she was being insecure, he decided, though he had no intention of telling her so. Something told him that "cute" would definitely be an unsavory four-letter word to Autumn Reed.

She was so beautiful. And so uncomfortable with that beauty. She had been much more confident in her work clothes and cap than she was now in this ultra-feminine dress. An unusual woman. And yet so very fascinating.

"Pull over for a minute, will you, Autumn?" he asked on a sudden impulse.

She glanced at him with a frown. "What?" she asked as if she hadn't heard him clearly.

"Pull over. Just for a minute," he repeated.

Her frown remained, but she gave a slight shrug and signaled a lane change, turning into the Saturday-deserted parking lot of an office building. Shifting into park, she turned slightly in her seat to face him. "Okay. Now what?"

"I just want to tell you that you're the most beautiful woman I've ever seen, your dress is fabulous and I'd like nothing more than to slowly peel it off you. But," he added as a wave of scarlet tinged her fair cheeks, "I'll settle for this for now."

He caught her face in his hands and brought his mouth firmly down on hers, kissing her as he'd wanted to do since he'd opened his door to find her standing there daring him to touch her.

Autumn stiffened for a moment—only a moment—and then leaned into him, her hands settling on his shoulders. Her lips parted beneath his, an invitation he accepted with alacrity. And then she was a whole-hearted participant in the kiss, and Jeff moaned softly at the pleasure of it. His pulse was roaring in his ears, his heart pounding against the walls of his chest when he finally drew back. He blinked rapidly a time or two, cleared his throat, took a deep breath, then nodded. "Okay. Now that's out of the way and we can enjoy ourselves. Where are we going for dinner?"

Autumn's eyes drifted slowly open, and the dazed expression in their green depths almost had him reaching out for her again. And then she gave a slight shake of her head, wet her lips and glared at him. "Why did you do that?" she demanded aggressively, her tone almost making him laugh. Now *this* was the Autumn he'd met three times before—arrogant, annoyed, regally self-assured. He liked her this way. He strongly suspected that he was beginning to love her this way.

"I wanted to," he answered her question, tongue in cheek as he prepared himself for her blistering response.

Instead, she turned sharply back to the steering wheel, slamming the car into drive and muttering something that sounded a lot like "obnoxious, conceited male." He did laugh then, earning himself a fulminating glance and a toss of auburn hair. But he had accomplished what he'd wanted, because she loosened up and began to reply when he made innocuous conversation. By the time they reached the popular, expensive restaurant where she'd been fortunate enough to obtain reservations for the evening, they were chatting away in relative ease. She'd been expecting him to pounce on her, he had, and now they could get on with the evening. Jeff was quite proud of himself for handling that particular situation so deftly.

Except his hands were still shaking in the aftermath of the most powerful kiss in his entire life.

"Tell me about yourself," he encouraged her when they'd ordered their dinners.

"Like what?" she asked, immediately looking wary.

He wondered what it was that could turn such a simple request into a threat to her. Why should she immediately go on the defensive just because he wanted to get to know her? "Anything," he answered simply. "Where you were born and when, whether you have any brothers and sisters, how you decided to become an electrician, when you moved to Florida, what flavor of ice cream you like, what you wear to bed."

The last suggestion made her blink, then glare at him before speaking quickly. "I was born twenty-five years ago in Rose Bud, Arkansas. My parents had three daughters in just over three years—I'm the youngest. I moved to Little Rock when I was twenty, started working to become an electrician immediately because it looked interesting and I like working with my hands. I moved to Tampa almost a year ago. I like chocolate mint ice cream and I sleep in large T-shirts. Any other questions?"

Delighted, he grinned and nodded. "Thousands."

She sighed deeply, propped her elbows on the table and looked at him with exaggerated patience. "Shoot."

He laughed. "You're certainly being accommodating."

"You're the one who said you like to converse with your dates. Converse."

"Okay. What are yout sister's names, where do they live, what do they do and are they married? Are you an aunt?"

She shook her head, looking a bit dizzy. "Whatever happened to one question at a time?"

"Takes too long. Besides, you fielded the last series so well I thought I'd give it another shot."

"Fair enough. My oldest sister is Spring McEntire. She's an optometrist in Little Rock, Arkansas, and she's married to a psychologist named Clay."

Jeff nodded gravely. "Okay. Go on."

"My other sister, Summer Anderson, is twenty-six. She and her husband, Derek, live in Sausalito, California, where she's studying to teach theater arts, and he's a business consultant. Did I answer them all?"

Laughing, Jeff shook his head. "No, you missed one. Are you an aunt?"

"Not yet. Summer and Derek had their first wedding anniversary last month, and Spring and Clay were married three months ago. I think both couples want children, though, when they decide the time is right."

"Do you?"

"Do I what?" she asked absently, toying with a bread stick because she knew what he was asking.

"Do you want children?"

She shrugged. "It's not high on my list of priorities."

"What is?"

Again a shrug preceded an answer that was just a bit too flip. "Independence. Self-sufficiency. Pride."

"Interesting answers."

"Yes, aren't they? Good thing you're a pediatrician instead of a shrink or you'd be busy trying to find out what makes me tick, wouldn't you?"

His gaze held hers. "I've been doing that from the moment we met, Autumn Reed."

She lowered her eyes, staring hard at the tablecloth. "Don't. I don't like being analyzed."

She was grateful that their dinners arrived just then. By the time they'd been served, Jeff had changed the subject, as if sensing that he'd better keep the conversation fairly impersonal if he wanted her to participate. Still, he continued to ask about things that related to her, unwilling to abandon his efforts to find out more about her. "Spring, Summer and Autumn. Pretty names, but you must have been teased quite a bit when you and your sisters were growing up."

She grimaced good-naturedly. "Did we ever. To make it worse, our father owns Reed's Seed and Feed Store in Rose Bud. Name games became our personal peeves. For a while we tried to change over to our middle names, Deborah, Linda and Sarah, but it never seemed to take. We were already firmly established as Spring, Summer and Autumn by that time."

"Autumn suits you," Jeff commented quietly, his gaze lingering on her red-brown hair, green eyes and gold-dusted dress.

She didn't quite know what to say to that, so she deftly turned the conversation back to him. "My turn to ask questions?"

He spread his hands in a go-ahead gesture.

"Where were you born and when, do you have any brothers and sisters, why did you decide to become a doctor, what's your favorite flavor of ice cream and what do you sleep in?" Autumn asked boldly.

He chuckled, then made an effort to answer in the correct order. "Born in Sarasota thirty-three years ago in July. No brothers or sisters. I wanted to be a doctor because it looked interesting and I like working with my hands." This was a teasing paraphrase from her. "My favorite flavor of ice cream is cherry vanilla, and I sleep in cotton pajamas."

Autumn choked on a sip of wine and looked suspiciously at him. "You really sleep in cotton pajamas?"

"Mmm. Want to find out for yourself?" he inquired mildly.

"I'll take your word for it," she muttered, though she was disconcerted to find herself flashing a mental image of unbuttoning the top to a set of cotton pajamas, a set being worn by a handsome, dark-haired doctor. *Behave yourself*, she crossly told her overactive imagination. "Has anyone ever told you that you're just a little too good to be true?" she casually asked the handsome, dark-haired doctor of her fantasy.

Jeff looked startled—and not altogether pleased. "What do you mean by that?"

Even to her, her smile was a bit feline. "You're a good-looking, single young doctor living in the nicest part of town in an immaculately kept home that you vacuum yourself. You're kind to children and electricians, you're every mother's dream of a polite gentleman, you have no vices that I've noticed—" he'd even turned down wine in favor of iced tea for dinner "—you don't mind if a woman asks you out or picks you up for a date, and you don't sleep in your underwear. You're darned near perfect, Jefferson Bradford."

She'd managed to make him blush, a fact she noted with a certain malicious pleasure. After all, she'd blushed a few times over him, and she hadn't liked it a bit!

"I'm hardly perfect, Autumn," he protested, still visibly embarrassed.

"Oh, yeah? Name a fault, then," she challenged him, beginning to enjoy this new game.

"I've been wanting to take you to bed since the moment I saw you, and it was all I could do not to throw you over my shoulder and haul you to my bedroom when I saw you in that dress tonight." His tone was brisk, answering her challenge in kind.

Proudly *not* blushing, she waved a hand in dismissal. "That's not a fault, it's a genetic weakness. You're a male, after all, and some things you can't help. Like breathing, eating and thinking with your hormones at times. What else?"

If he'd hoped to disconcert her, he was disappointed, but he made a valiant effort to prove himself imperfect. "I don't like cats."

She shook her head. "Lots of people don't like cats," she returned. "That doesn't count, either. What else?"

He exhaled gustily. "I was hoping I wouldn't have to tell you this."

Crossing her hands in front of her, she leaned forward, her lips curving into an avid smile. "Tell. Tell."

He looked one way and then the other, furtively, obviously checking for eavesdroppers. And then, very quietly, "I'm an addict."

He'd spoken so seriously that Autumn was taken aback. An addict? She'd read about doctors who took advantage of their access to drugs, but Jeff? No way. "You are not."

He nodded gravely. "Yes, I am. It started in medical school, and now I can't stop. I'm truly hooked."

"On *what*?" she demanded, beginning to get concerned.

"*Dr. Wilson's World*," he replied mournfully, looking deeply ashamed.

Autumn relaxed muscles that she hadn't deliberately tensed and semiseriously considered decorating his pin-striped suit with the remains of her dinner. "A soap opera? You're hooked on a soap?"

Still looking as if he'd confessed to a string of heinous crimes, he nodded. "For years. I tape it every day and watch it before bedtime or on weekends. I can't help it. When I miss it, I start wondering what's happening to Paul or Melanie or Dan or Misty or poor old Dr. Wilson, and I'm not satisfied until I find out."

"That's appalling."

"I know." He hung his head in shame.

"You know it will rot your brain."

He nodded, chin sinking even lower. Then he risked an upward glance at her though his lush dark lashes—much too lush for a man, she thought enviously—and his blue eyes were dancing with humor. "Now will you believe I'm not perfect?"

"I suppose I'll have to. Anyone who watches *Dr. Wilson's World* every day is seriously flawed."

"I can't help it," he repeated, looking quite pleased with himself. "I'm compulsive."

"I'm terribly disillusioned. So tell me, who do you think is the father of Misty's baby? Dan? Running Wolf? Or old Dr. Wilson?"

Jeff shouted with laughter, not at all concerned that dozens of eyes immediately turned his way. "You watch it, too!" he accused her in what could only be termed unholy glee.

She lifted her chin disdainfully. "Not very often, but when I do, it's for a good reason."

"Oh, yeah? What?"

"I like to watch Dr. Noble suffer."

Jeff eyed her questioningly, obviously confused by her pleasure in the many tribulations suffered by the serial's unfortunate heartthrob hero, one of the more popular actors on daytime TV. "You mean you're a fan of his?"

"Nope," she answered cheerfully. "I keep hoping he'll die in a horrible soap opera accident and fade into television oblivion. No such luck so far, but hope lives on."

"I don't suppose you want to explain?"

"Nope," she replied, deciding not to tell him that the actor who played Dr. Noble was a Little Rock native who'd painfully jilted her sister, Summer, after her permanently damaging motorcycle accident. "But I *am* glad you have a weakness. I have so many myself that you were making me feel inferior."

"Name a few."

She shook her head firmly. "Subject closed. Tell me about doctoring."

So they talked about him for a while, about the grueling course of study in medical school, the exhausting hours of internship and residency, the occasional heartbreak and more frequent rewards, the demands on time and energy. And Autumn listened in fascination, feeling herself growing more and more attracted to him—if that were possible—as the evening went on. And then they were talking about her again, and she was telling him funny stories about her work and discussing favorite books and movies and television programs, and too soon their dinner was over.

Dancing seemed to be the natural continuation of their evening, a physical confirmation of the intimacy that had begun when they'd both confessed to watching the same soap opera. While they were dancing, she discovered the small electronic pager attached to his belt, reminding her of his demanding profession. "Are you on call?" she asked.

"No. I always carry the beeper in case Pam or Julian need to contact me. They know I want to be notified if anything serious happens to one of my patients, even though whoever is on call is perfectly capable of taking care of any situation."

A dedicated man. A very special man. How could she possibly resist him?

Autumn loved to dance, and Jeff was the perfect partner. She could have quite happily remained in his arms for days, their feet moving in easy synchronization, their conversation light and low-voiced, his hand warm on her bare back.

"I love this dress," Jeff informed her, as if reading her thoughts.

"Thank you. I'm glad Webb made me wear it," she murmured, drifting along in some wonderful fantasy, barely conscious of what she'd said.

But Jeff heard her, and he stiffened. "Webb?" he asked, a bit too casually.

"Webb." She lifted her head from Jeff's shoulder and smiled up at him. "Webb's one of my best friends. You know him—Webb Brothers. He says you go to the same health club."

"Sure, I know him. Nice guy. In fact, he's the reason I called your company when I needed an electrician. I like to do business with my friends when I can. Are you and he, uh . . . ?"

"Friends," she supplied firmly, choosing to leave it at that. After all, she didn't owe Jeff any explanations.

"Are you involved with anyone else? Seriously, I mean," Jeff asked cautiously.

She shouldn't really answer. She wouldn't. He shouldn't even have asked. But then her mouth opened, and the words came out on their own. "No, I'm not involved with anyone. And I like it that way."

"I'm not, either," he told her, returning the courtesy, even though she hadn't asked. "But I don't know that I like it that way. It's just the way things are right now."

He was a man who would want a wife and a family, a man who was probably looking for those things now that he'd established his career as a doctor. Autumn dropped her eyes to the knot in his tie, reminding herself once again that she had no business being out with this man, feeling these feelings for this man. She was single servings, irregular hours and haphazard housekeeping; he was dinner at eight, family outings and socks in the hamper. She belonged to a union and a bowler's league; he joined community service organizations and health clubs. They were opposite ends of the spectrum, day and night, apples and oranges.

And his hand on her back was turning her into marshmallow.

She stifled a sigh and swayed to the strains of romantic music, memorizing the feel of his chest pressed lightly against her breasts, his thighs brushing hers, his arms around her, his breath on her forehead. No, she couldn't allow herself to become too deeply involved with him. It wouldn't work. He deserved someone who could give more, who wanted to give more.

But, Lord, she wanted him! The sensual side of herself that she'd sternly repressed for the past few years responded to him in a way that she'd responded to no man before him, not even Steven. She was tormented by images, images that had formed in her mind the moment she'd met him. His head bent to hers, his hand on her thigh, his mouth at her breast. Her hands buried deep in his luxurious ebony hair, her lips tasting the firm, glistening skin of his chest. She groaned softly.

"Did you say something?" Jeff asked, still moving in a slow, tantalizing dance.

"No," she assured him without looking up.

An affair. The modern, sophisticated thing to do would be to have an affair with him. An affair that she controlled—taken at her own speed, ended when she was ready. The ultimate in liberation. She wanted him, he'd indicated that he wanted her. Why not? She'd learned years before that sex and marriage—even sex and love—did not necessarily have to go together. Consenting adults did it every day—met, acknowledged mutual attraction, slept together and parted, unscarred by the experience. She was twenty-five, no longer an innocent small-town girl in the throes of infatuation. She could handle it.

Couldn't she?

Of course she could.

The music ended. Jeff stepped back and smiled at her. Her heart jumped into her throat.

Then again, maybe she couldn't.

"WOULD YOU LIKE to come in?"

"Um, I don't think so. It's late." Autumn had the oddest sense of postponing the inevitable as she declined Jeff's invitation, but she still felt compelled to try.

"Could you spare just a minute? I'd like your advice on something."

She looked at him suspiciously, finding his expression blandly innocent in the murky light inside her car. "What?"

"Pool lights, remember?" He sounded surprised that she hadn't known. "I told you that I'd like your advice on redoing them."

"At—" she squinted at the lighted clock on her dashboard "—one o'clock in the morning?"

He lifted one shoulder in a half shrug. "If you're too tired, it's okay. I understand. We'll do it another time."

With an inward sigh at her own lack of judgment, Autumn reached for her door handle. "All right, I'll look at it," she told him, swinging her legs out from under the steering wheel. Of course she didn't believe that Jeff had invited her in only to look at his pool, but then, that wasn't her purpose for going in with him, either.

It might be the dumbest thing she'd ever done, she decided, but the past couple of hours spent dancing in Jeff's arms had left her hungry for more of him. She'd made her token protest to salve her own conscience later; now she was giving in to desire and curiosity. After five years of caution and control she figured she owed herself one evening of impulsive pleasure.

Without speaking, Jeff led her straight through his house—as immaculate as she remembered it—and then through double glass doors to the screened-in patio containing his pool. Glancing almost indifferently around her, Autumn briefly noted the romantically subdued lighting, tastefully contemporary patio furniture and lush profusion of tropical plants before turning immediately back to Jeff. At that moment she had no interest in anything but him.

Jeff stared back at her, his hands in his pockets, his face carefully shuttered, but his eyes glowing with what could only be interpreted as hunger. A hunger to equal hers. Autumn locked suddenly icy fingers in front of her, her heart beginning to pound.

"So, uh—" he strengthened his voice with a visible effort "—what do you think?"

"About what?" she asked in little more than a whisper. Even that small sound seemed to reverberate in the middle-of-the-night stillness surrounding them, isolating them.

"The lights." He gestured awkwardly with one hand, the movement meant to include the entire patio.

"I think they're perfect." For just this little while, Autumn thought, everything was perfect. The evening, the setting, the mood. The man. She ached for him to touch her.

His gaze holding hers, Jeff took a slow step forward. And then another. And then she was in his arms, and finally he was kissing her as she'd longed for him to kiss her, as she'd dreaded for him to kiss her. Even as she gave herself up to the devastating effects of the embrace, she tried to convince herself that one kiss could not change her entire life.

Jeff swallowed a groan as his hold tightened convulsively around the beautiful woman in his arms. He told himself that her passionate response shouldn't come as a surprise, but it did. He hadn't expected such glorious enthusiasm.

Her arms were around his neck, her full breasts crushed against his chest. Her bare back was warm and yielding beneath his eager palms, making him ravenous for more of her. He swept the depths of her mouth, savoring the sweet taste of her. Her tongue welcomed his, and this time he couldn't hold back his groan of pleasure.

Desire had never come so swiftly, need so powerfully. Jeff wanted her so desperately that he thought he would shatter into dust if he couldn't have her. He ached, he throbbed with desire for her. Inside his head, his chest. His arms, his legs. The painfully swollen part of him that was even now pressing into her stomach. He groaned again when she moved closer, her body undulating sinuously against him.

"Autumn," he muttered against her lips, needing to say her name. It felt so good on his tongue that he said it again. "Autumn."

Her fingers toyed with the hair at the back of his neck. He shivered, burying his face in her softly scented throat, tasting the glistening skin there. She arched her neck for him, allowing him freer access. He pressed another kiss to her throat, then lifted his head, wanting to look at her.

God, she was so beautiful. Her fair skin was flushed with passion, her hair tousled and shining in the golden patio lighting. Lips kiss-darkened, eyes closed, lashes lying softly against her cheeks. Everything in her pose and expression told him that she was more than willing to increase the intimacy of their embraces. All he had to do was lead her inside, unfasten the button of that stunning dress and he could have her. At last.

5

JEFF BROKE into a cold sweat, his body tensing in protest at what he had to do. Somehow, from somewhere, he had to find the strength to step away from her. For he knew without a doubt that if he took her now, he would lose her.

She was offering her body, her passion. An affair, glorious though temporary. He wanted her love. Her future. Everything she had to give. He wanted to offer the same. But she wasn't ready to give or receive love. Only passion. And, God help him, that wasn't enough. He'd thought it would be, but it wasn't.

Taking a deep breath that burned its way into his lungs, he reached up with trembling hands and removed her arms from around his neck. Reluctantly he stepped back toward the glass doors that led into his house. Unaware that he was bringing the evening to an end, Autumn gave him a sultry smile that went straight to his clenched stomach. She spread her slender fingers across his chest, then leaned forward to plant a butterfly kiss on his jaw.

Jeff almost whimpered. But then he brought himself sternly under control and took her wrists in his hands, turning to walk inside with her. He didn't pause in the den but kept walking, straight to the front door. "I had a wonderful time tonight, Autumn," he told her, unable to make his voice sound completely normal. "Thank you."

Her expression stunned, Autumn blinked and looked up at him as if she couldn't quite believe she was hearing him correctly. "I had a good time, too," she said finally, "but—"

Jeff reached for the doorknob, avoiding her eyes. "Drive carefully, okay? After all, it *is* late."

"It's not *that* late," she replied curtly, and he could see confusion turning to annoyance in her emerald eyes. He could deal with her anger later, he assured himself, resisting an urge to cross his fingers.

"It's after one. And I'm on call tomorrow," he told her, deliberately casual. He dropped a light kiss on her unresponsive lips, smiled brightly, bade her good-night and politely closed the door in her astonished face.

He leaned weakly against that door for a moment before turning abruptly and heading back to the pool, shedding his clothes as he went and leaving them strewn behind him. He was halfway into his first lap before the sound of Autumn's Fiero faded into the distance. He lost count of the laps long before he crawled out of the pool, quivering with exhaustion but still taut with frustration.

AUTUMN STARED at Jeff's front door for a full minute before closing her mouth, spinning on one high heel and stalking to her car. She slid behind the wheel and slammed the door but could not bring herself to start the engine immediately. Instead, she sat in dazed silence, trying to decide what had just happened.

Jeff had thrown her out! First he'd kissed her like she'd never been kissed before, made her want him like she'd never wanted anyone, then he'd thrown her out! Slammed the door in her face, left her standing on the doorstep like . . . like a cat he was putting out for the night, she thought indignantly. A person could get whiplash from that abrupt a reversal!

Wouldn't you know it, she thought glumly, eventually reaching out to turn the key in the ignition. *I finally decide I'm mature enough and sophisticated enough to handle a brief affair, and I have to choose a genuine, old-time Southern gentleman who won't take a woman to bed on the first date.*

At least she assumed that Jeff had considered he was being courteous by ending their intimate interlude so unsatisfactorily. She would never believe that he hadn't wanted her as badly as she wanted him. After all, she'd been pressed as closely against him as possible while they were still wearing clothes. The man had definitely been interested. Remembering the solid, heavy feel of him, she shivered with another ripple of desire. How could he leave her this way? she wailed silently, shifting uncomfortably on the vinyl seat.

It was during the cold shower she took before turning in that she decided she wanted Jeff Bradford, dammit, and she was going to have him! How dare he think that he was the one responsible for deciding how far their relationship would go, and at what rate it would proceed! She was a woman of the eighties, fully capable of deciding for herself whom she would sleep with and when. And though she had no intention of becoming seriously involved with Jeff, she would admit to being very attracted to him and willing, if not eager, to pursue that attraction to its logical conclusion. One night, a few weeks, perhaps even a few months, and they could go their own ways, Jeff to continue his search for a suitable doctor's wife and Autumn to continue to work toward owning her own company.

Curled on the bed beside Babs a few minutes later, Autumn closed her eyes and tried to will herself to sleep. But memories of being held in Jeff's arms, being kissed and caressed by him, continued to plague her until she groaned and buried her face in her pillow. She would make him pay for this, she thought vengefully. And she'd make him enjoy every minute of his punishment. Just as she would.

JEFF LIFTED the feverish toddler from the examining table and snuggled him for a moment against his shoulder. "Poor little fella," he murmured for his tiny patient's ears. "You really feel rotten, don't you? Well, that medicine I just prescribed is going to make you feel better almost immediately, so just don't you worry about it, you hear?"

With one last pat on the lethargic little boy's diapered bottom, he passed the child to his mother, who smiled sweetly at him. "You are so wonderful with children, Dr. Bradford," she told him gratefully. "You really should have some of your own."

"I'm working on it, Mrs. Evans," he replied cheerfully as he escorted her to the door, a hazy image of a child with red hair and emerald eyes flitting through his mind. Then he mentally laughed at himself for being an incurable optimist. At this point he'd be lucky to get another date with Autumn, and here he was fantasizing about having children with her!

Still thinking of Autumn, he sat behind the massive desk in his office and reached for his tape recorder to dictate diagnosis and treatment for the file of the child he'd just examined. He'd just snapped the recorder on when he was interrupted by Pam's appearance in the doorway. "Well?" she demanded, crossing her arms over her chest and leaning against his desk.

Jeff turned the recorder off. "Well, what?"

Pam sighed impatiently. "Have you called her yet?"

He knew who she meant, of course, but he couldn't help teasing her a bit longer. Pam was so teasable. "Have I called who yet?"

"Darn it, Jeff, you know who! Autumn! Now tell me, have you?"

"No, Pam, I haven't called her," he answered, relenting.

"Well, why not? This is Friday! If you're going to ask her out for this weekend, you'd better get busy. She's probably got plans already. Or are you waiting for her to call you?"

"I'll call her as soon as I get home this evening," Jeff assured his partner, throwing an arm over the back of his desk chair as he smiled at her. "Now are you satisfied?"

She shook her head, her brown curls bobbing with the motion. "I still don't understand why you waited so long to call her when I can tell you've been just dying to do so all week. What do you want to bet she's already got a date for tomorrow night?"

"Then I'll ask her out for another night," he answered logically. "Believe me, Pam, I have my reasons."

"Yes, you told me your reasons. Some garbage about her having to chase after you if you're going to catch her. That's not the way things were done in my day! Back then it was the men who did the chasing and the women loved it."

Jeff laughed, eyeing the indignant surgeon with fond amusement. Having put herself through medical

school, graduating at the top of her class, Pam was
hardly the unassuming Southern belle she was imitating. He wondered what had gotten into her lately. "Pamela, you sound like a little old lady. In your day,
indeed. You've only been married for two years, remember? And according to Bob, you did a bit of chasing yourself. Weren't you the one who rammed your car
into his once when you were dating so he couldn't leave
having the last word in an argument?"

"That's different," Pam returned dismissively, waving one hand in the air.

"I thought you'd think so," Jeff murmured.

"Dr. Bradford, your next patient is here. And Dr.
Cochran, you have a telephone call. It's Dr. Neville
from Tampa General."

"Thanks, Sheila. I'll take it in my office." With one
last frowning look at Jeff Pam turned and marched out
of the room, leaving him grinning and shaking his head
as he pushed himself away from his desk and went off
to take care of his next patient.

He hoped he was doing the right thing by treating
Autumn so casually. Every day for the past week he'd
fought the urge to call her, reminding himself over and
over that she wouldn't appreciate his chasing her too
fervently. He'd told himself that he would be the pursued, he thought as he entered the examining room in
which his patient was waiting. He only hoped the attraction between them was strong enough for Autumn
to remain interested.

"SO," EMILY ASKED with suspicious nonchalance, "have
you heard from your friend lately?"

Thinking that Emily could only be referring to Jeff, Autumn shook her head and glared down at her dinner plate. "No. Not since our date last Saturday."

"Oh, I didn't mean Jeff," Emily corrected her quickly, dabbing at Ryan's mouth with a napkin to remove a smear of the broccoli he was happily eating with his fingers. "I meant your friend Webb."

Autumn arched an eyebrow and looked across her dining table at her neighbor, who had joined Autumn for an early dinner followed by a television special they both wanted to see. So Emily was interested in Webb, was she? Autumn grinned, remembering that Webb had casually inquired about Emily on at least three different occasions during the past week since he'd met her. "Of course I've heard from Webb, Emily. I work with him, remember? I see him every day."

"Oh, of course." Emily flushed a bit and focused her china-blue eyes on the broiled fish fillet in front of her. "How silly of me."

Autumn chuckled. "Emily, if you're interested in Webb, just come out and say so. What would you like to know about him?"

Blushing deeper, Emily smiled sheepishly and looked at Autumn. "Everything. I thought he was nice. And so handsome! I'm surprised that you're not dating him yourself."

"Webb and I are just friends. We're too much alike to be anything else," Autumn explained. "He's a great guy, but he's been known to break a few hearts. He claims to be allergic to commitment."

"It does sound like the two of you are a lot alike," Emily agreed in amusement. "Ryan, don't rub your Jell-O in your hair!"

Laughing at Ryan's antics, Autumn turned back to her dinner. As she finished, she told Emily how she'd met Webb, then shared some funny stories of escapades she and Webb had been involved in during the past months. Privately she thought that Emily and Webb would make a good couple. She suspected that Emily would be the type who'd adore and admire the man she loved, and Webb was one of those males who'd enjoy the adulation and return it in full measure once he'd accepted the inevitable. He loved kids, so Ryan wouldn't be a problem.

If only the man weren't so shy of serious involvement, Autumn mused, not finding it at all strange that she was in favor of marriage for Webb when she was so wary of the institution for herself. It wasn't marriage itself that she opposed, but the fear of losing herself within the bonds of such a union. Others seemed to handle the responsibilities just fine—her own two sisters were embarrassingly happy in their wedded states. But Autumn's too-close encounter had left her decidedly marriage-shy.

Thoughts of Jeff Bradford tried to creep into her mind, but she firmly closed a mental door against them, telling herself that there was absolutely no connection between her reflections on marriage and the man who'd shattered her peace of mind in the six weeks since she'd met him. She'd been expecting Jeff to call all week. Not that she'd made any special effort to stay close to her phone because of that, she assured herself. She'd simply had several things to do that had kept her home every night that week.

"Webb sure left in a hurry when I told him that I was divorced," Emily said with a sigh as they stood to carry their plates into the kitchen. "Has he got something against divorcées?"

Bringing her thoughts back to their conversation with an effort, Autumn shook her head at Emily's question. "No. He only runs like that when he meets a woman who could become a threat to his bachelorhood."

Emily frowned at that, then slowly smiled. "Oh. I see."

Autumn returned the smile. "I thought you would. Maybe I'll ask him over one night next week. I could use some help with the bookcase that I want to move from the living room to my bedroom."

"I think that sounds like an excellent idea," Emily agreed, her eyes dancing. "Oh, Autumn, I'm glad I met you. I've been lonely since Earl and I divorced. He'd pretty well alienated all our friends with his drinking by the time we split up, and I've been reluctant to get back in touch with them. It's nice to have a friend again."

Autumn reached into a cabinet for a cookie for Ryan's dessert, pleased by Emily's words. "I'm glad we met, too," she admitted. "Until you came along, I hadn't realized that almost all my friends in Tampa are men that I work with. It's nice to have a woman to talk to again."

Emily started to say something, then paused as the telephone rang. "Maybe that's Jeff," she said eagerly, confirming Autumn's suspicion that Emily knew how much Autumn had been hoping he'd call, even though Autumn had said very little about Jeff to Emily.

Though her heart had begun to pound—as it had each time the telephone had rung during the past week, to Autumn's disgust—she tried to sound as if she didn't really care that Jeff might be the caller. "Could be. Excuse me, Emily."

She picked up the receiver of the yellow kitchen wall phone. "Hello?"

"Hello, Autumn."

Jeff. "Hi," she said a little too breathlessly, then nodded at Emily to confirm that it was, indeed, him. "If you want to go ahead and get comfortable in the living room, I'll join you in a few minutes," she told her grinning friend before turning her full attention back to the telephone call. "How are you, Jeff?"

"You have company?" he asked without answering her perfunctory question. "I can call back another time if it's not convenient now."

Noting the displeasure in his voice with mixed feelings, Autumn wound the telephone cord around her finger. "No, it's okay. I can talk for a few minutes. Emily and Ryan had dinner with me, and we're going to watch a television special together."

"Emily and Ryan?"

"My neighbor and her fifteen-month-old son. I thought I'd mentioned them at dinner last week."

"Yeah, I think you did," Jeff agreed, his voice suddenly sounding brighter. "What television program are you going to watch?" he inquired, obviously reluctant to end the call.

"The magician Jeremy Kane has his first TV special on tonight. The television guide said he was going to do some pretty spectacular illusions."

"You like magic?"

"Yes. And Jeremy Kane is one of my favorite magicians. I'd love to see him perform in person someday."

"I'll keep that in mind. Actually, though, I called to see if you'd like to go out with me tomorrow night. Unless you have other plans, of course."

The awkwardness of the invitation was somehow endearing. Autumn tried to steel herself against the softness he brought out in her even as she accepted. "No, I don't have any other plans for tomorrow night. I'd like to go out with you."

"Great." He didn't try to hide his pleasure. "I thought we'd do something casual this time, so don't dress up, okay?"

"Fine. Sounds like fun." She noted absently that the end of her finger was turning purple as the tightly wound telephone cord cut off her circulation.

"Seven o'clock?"

"All right."

"Autumn?"

"Yes, Jeff?"

"I need your address."

"Oh, of course." She gave it to him, listened as he carefully repeated the numbers, then hung up when he did. Unwrapping her purple finger, she stood absently rubbing it, her gaze unseeingly on the telephone. Funny, she thought, she hadn't even hesitated to accept the date. After a week of indecision, alternating between never wanting to see him again and fighting the urge to chase him down and drag him into bed, she'd meekly accepted his invitation when he'd finally gotten around to calling her. And she'd quickly explained who was with her when she could sense that he thought he'd interrupted a more intimate evening. If she wasn't careful, she thought with a weak attempt at humor, Jeff Bradford was going to have her involved with him before she even knew it.

Only the thought wasn't at all funny. That was exactly what she was worried about.

"Hello in there." Emily's voice held amusement as she broke into Autumn's deep reverie.

Autumn looked sheepishly at the doorway where Emily watched her with a smile. "Uh, that was Jeff."

"I know. Did he ask you out again?"

"Yes. Tomorrow night."

"You *are* going, aren't you?"

"Yes, I'm going."

"Good." Emily's smile broadened. "I think this man is good for you."

"No." Autumn shook her head emphatically. "He's all wrong for me. Exactly the opposite of the kind of man I usually date."

"That's what I meant. He's good for you." With that smug comment Emily turned toward the living room. "Jeremy Kane's about to come on. We don't want to miss his opening illusion."

Pulling two canned soft drinks out of the refrigerator, Autumn followed her friend, knowing as she did so that it was going to be hard to lose herself in the performer's illusions when her mind would be so fully filled with memories of Jeff. She was beginning to believe that Jeff Bradford possessed a few magic powers of his own. She could only assume that she had been bewitched.

AUTUMN SPENT quite a bit less time worrying about clothes for her second date with Jeff than she had for her first. After all, if "that gold thing"—the most powerful weapon in her wardrobe arsenal—hadn't overcome Jeff's strong willpower, no garment would. Still, she took pains to look her best in a vividly patterned, short-sleeved camp shirt and pleated khaki slacks, her thick, curling hair confined at the back of her head with a banana clip. Bold plastic earrings, a heavy matching bracelet and bright green flats completed her colorful outfit. She had just finished applying her makeup when her doorbell rang, some fifteen minutes before seven. Either Jeff was early or . . .

"Webb." She sighed as she opened her door. "What are you doing here?"

He grinned in pure enjoyment. "Making trouble."

"So what else is new? Go away, Webb."

"Nope." Looking as attractive as always in a fashionably casual shirt and slacks, he strolled past her and dropped onto her couch, draping himself comfortably across the pillows as if he were prepared to stay for a while. Absently patting Babs when she jumped up to greet him, he looked at Autumn. "What time's Bradford supposed to be here?"

"How do you know I've got a date with Jeff?" Autumn demanded in frustration.

"Call it a lucky guess. I was right, wasn't I?"

"Yes, you were right. Now will you go away? He's supposed to be here in fifteen minutes."

"I thought I'd say hello. I haven't seen him in a while. Got a beer?"

Autumn started to tell him exactly what he could do with himself—an anatomical impossibility—but then she paused as a mischievous thought crossed her mind. She'd teach Webb not to play games with her, she decided abruptly. He *deserved* to find himself waiting at the altar. But not with her. "Sure, I've got a beer. I'll get you one," she told him, smiling sweetly as she headed for the kitchen.

Webb straightened on the couch, watching her leave with a frown at her suspicious acquiescence. "What are you planning, Autumn?"

"I'm not planning anything, Webb," she assured him over her shoulder. "I just know when to accept the inevitable. You're not going to disappear until Jeff gets here, are you?"

"Nope."

"So I won't waste my time pleading with you. Don't you have a date tonight?" she asked, raising her voice to be heard in the other room as she rummaged in the refrigerator for a beer.

"Not tonight," Webb called back. "Thought I'd head over to Charlie's later and check out the scenery." Charlie's was a popular singles' bar that Webb liked to frequent. Autumn hated the place she always called the "meat market."

She picked up the phone and quickly punched in her neighbor's number. "Emily? Hi, it's Autumn. Can you come over for a minute? Yeah, right now. Make up an excuse, will you? Webb's here, and Jeff's supposed to arrive any minute. If you're here, too, Webb just might behave himself." The conversation was brief and low-voiced. Autumn was smiling when she hung up.

Webb had barely popped the top of his beer when the doorbell rang. He lifted his eyebrows in a devilish expression. "Lover-boy's here."

"Webb, why do you find it so amusing that I'm going out with Jeff?" Autumn asked curiously, knowing who was at the door.

He lifted one shoulder, grinning unrepentantly. "Maybe it's because I didn't think there was anyone who could rattle that tough, cool exterior of yours. I'm pleased to know that Ms Autumn Reed has a few insecurities like the rest of us mere mortals."

Shaking her head in exasperation, Autumn opened the door, winking at Emily. "Hello, Emily. Hi, Ryan," she said clearly, amused as Webb coughed on a sip of beer behind her. "Come in."

"Thanks. I brought the sweater you wanted to borrow." Her blue eyes twinkling with suppressed laughter, Emily held out a thin red oversized sweater that Autumn had once admired.

Grateful that the sweater just happened to match the outfit she'd chosen to wear, Autumn draped it over her arm. "Thanks, Emily. I'd heard a cold front was supposed to come through later and I didn't have a thing to wear with this blouse. You remember Webb, don't you?"

Autumn hadn't realized that her neighbor had any talent in the dramatic arts, but Emily's look of pleased surprise was superb. "Of course I do. Hello, Webb. How nice to see you again."

Immediately on his feet, Webb managed a smile, trying very hard to keep his eyes on Emily's lovely face instead of the creamy cleavage revealed by her scoop-necked ice-blue sweater. He wasn't entirely successful, Autumn noted with malicious pleasure. "Hello, Emily," he said faintly.

From his usual position on his mother's hip, Ryan smiled happily at Webb and held out his chubby hands, babbling a welcome in his mostly incomprehensible toddler dialect. "I think he remembers you," Emily remarked, giving Webb one of her guaranteed-to-daze-any-red-blooded-male smiles.

Predictably dazed, Webb lifted Ryan into his arms and grinned besottedly down at the sandy-haired imp. "Yeah, I think he does. How's it going, buddy?"

"He's been active lately," Emily told him with a smile. "He's practicing his climbing. He's made it to the top of the bookcase twice now."

Webb laughed, his eyes drifting back to Emily's face . . . and the rest of her. "I'll bet he keeps you busy."

"Oh, he does. But I'm not complaining. He's a sweetheart."

"Does, uh, does he see his father very often?" Webb asked hesitantly, his gaze turning back to the child.

Emily's smile faded. "No. My ex-husband wasn't fond of children. Ryan was an accident. After the divorce Earl decided to write both of us off as mistakes. I haven't seen him or heard from him in a year."

Webb frowned. "What a jerk. How could any man walk away from his own son? Or from you?" he added slowly, looking once more at the beautiful young woman in front of him.

As Emily flushed in pleasure and retrieved her son, Autumn resisted the impulse to laugh out loud. *Oh, Webb, my friend, you're in big trouble*, she thought gleefully. *That'll teach you to make fun of me for being rattled by Jeff Bradford.* And then her amusement faded as she wondered if she wore the same expression around Jeff that Webb was currently wearing as he looked at Emily.

Bewitched, she thought again. *Maybe we're both bewitched.* A shiver of something very near fear coursed down her spine, and she was suddenly sorry that she'd found such amusement in almost throwing Emily at Webb. Was she to be paid back in kind?

When the doorbell rang again she jumped, earning herself a delighted grin from Webb, who was obviously not quite as distracted as Autumn had hoped.

Glaring at him, Autumn took a deep breath and opened the door, then promptly lost the breath in a soft whoosh as she took in the man smiling at her from the doorstep. He was dressed in a pale yellow crewneck sweater and light gray slacks, looking as devastatingly attractive as he had in his expensive suit the week before. Surely it wasn't possible that he grew more good-looking each time she saw him, she thought despairingly. His hair couldn't really have grown darker and thicker, his eyes bluer and warmer, his shoulders broader and more muscular. God, he was gorgeous!

"Hi, Jeff." Oh, hell. She'd sounded breathless again. Probably because she was.

"Hi, Autumn." His own voice was low, caressing, sending hot tremors through every inch of her body.

Clinging to the door, Autumn invited him in, waiting until he'd passed her to shut the door and lean weakly against it. "Jeff, you know Webb. And this is my neighbor, Emily Hinson, and her son, Ryan. Emily, this is Dr. Jeff Bradford."

Nodding a greeting at Webb, Jeff smiled at Emily. "Hi. Nice to meet you."

"You're a doctor?" Emily shot a reproving look at her friend. "Autumn didn't mention that."

"Jeff's a pediatrician," Autumn explained.

Emily looked interested. "You are? Where's your office? Ryan and I just moved here from St. Pete three months ago, and I haven't found a pediatrician for him in Tampa yet."

Jeff named his clinic and gave the address, adding that he had two partners. "Julian's a very good doctor, and Pam's a skilled surgeon," he explained. "We'd be happy to take care of this guy. Not that he doesn't look perfectly healthy." He grinned at Ryan, reaching out to ruffle the toddler's sandy hair. "Hello, Ryan. Aren't you a fine-looking fellow?"

Well, he just won Emily over, Autumn thought ruefully. She tried not to acknowledge that she was pleased that Jeff showed no signs of interest in Ryan's mother, other than polite friendliness. She would not admit that she'd been at all worried that Jeff might have exhibited the same weakness for Emily's delicate blond beauty that Webb had displayed.

Webb offered a hand to Jeff. "How's it going, Jeff? Haven't seen you in ages."

"It's good to see you again, Webb. Now that the clinic's open late on the same evenings the Jaycees meet, I don't have much chance to be active in the chapter."

"We appreciated your contribution last month to the project for handicapped kids. You were very generous." Webb waited until Jeff had modestly shrugged off the praise before shooting a mischievous look at Autumn. "So you're interested in Autumn, are you? Good luck, my friend. You've got nerve, I'll say that for you."

"Webb . . ." Autumn murmured threateningly as Jeff grinned at the other man.

"Can't say I blame you for trying, of course," Webb continued bravely. "But be warned, Bradford. She has the devil's own temper."

Autumn was showing signs of that temper as Emily stepped in quickly to defuse the situation. "I guess we'd better be going. It was nice to meet you, Dr. Bradford. See you tomorrow, Autumn." She turned a shamelessly limpid look at Webb. "Bye, Webb. Maybe I'll see you again sometime."

Immediately forgetting Autumn and Jeff, Webb seemed to struggle inwardly for about half a minute before blurting out, "Why don't we take Ryan out for ice cream, Emily? He *can* eat ice cream, can't he?"

"He loves ice cream," Emily replied happily. "Are you sure you didn't have any other plans for the evening?"

Perjuring himself without hesitation, Webb denied any plans for that evening. Autumn swallowed a chuckle as her friend deliberately chose an ice-cream parlor over Tampa's hottest night spot. She managed not to laugh until Webb had departed with Emily and Ryan, though she had no intention of keeping quiet about his choice next time she saw him.

"What's so funny?" Jeff asked quizzically, looking up from where he'd knelt to pat Babs.

Autumn decided not to enlighten him. Instead, she introduced him to Babs and went to get her purse so they could leave, suddenly conscious that the two of them were alone. The nervousness that had faded in her amusement at Webb's reluctant interest in Emily returned full force.

6

ANY NERVOUSNESS that Autumn may have experienced when the date began was long gone by the time she and Jeff had dined on hamburgers, chuckled through a new comedy film and then spent an hour in an arcade in friendly competition. It was as if Jeff deliberately made the date as unthreatening as possible to put her at ease. If so, his strategy worked. She had a marvelous time, laughing until her sides ached.

"Okay, lady, you asked for it. I'm breaking through your defenses this time, and there's nothing you can do to stop me." Jeff's threat was uttered in a growl, blue eyes narrowed with intent.

Autumn tensed in reaction, her own eyes returning the challenge. "Would you like to make a small wager on that?"

"I," he informed her loftily, "never bet on a sure thing. You may as well prepare to surrender."

"I," she returned haughtily, "never surrender. Give it your best shot, Bradford."

"Don't say I didn't warn you," he told her softly, then exploded into action. His arm swept in a powerful arc, the paddle in his hand sending the air hockey puck skimming across the table between them, heading straight for Autumn's goal.

Skillfully Autumn deflected the puck with a snap of her wrist, turning it back toward Jeff's goal. Over and over they returned the volley, each intent on scoring the winning point. And then Autumn happened to glance up at Jeff, taking her eyes away from the table to admire him with his face flushed, eyes bright, hair disheveled, dimples flashing—and promptly lost the game.

"All right!" Jeff leaped straight into the air, one arm waving above his head as he celebrated his victory, one of the few he'd managed since he and Autumn had wandered into the arcade over an hour ago.

"Don't gloat, Jeff. It's not becoming."

He grinned and looped an arm around her neck. "Oh, yeah? Who was gloating a few minutes ago after winning three straight games of Galactic Shoot-out? Who pointed out that she destroyed all my spaceships in the first ninety seconds of the first game? Who won the most tickets playing Skee-Ball? Who—"

"Okay, okay," Autumn interrupted, laughing. "So I gloated. Now it's your turn. Go ahead."

"I'm much too good a sport to gloat," Jeff answered with immense dignity, then added in a stage whisper, "Loser."

Autumn giggled and punched him in the ribs. Then she swallowed a moan as she realized that she had, indeed, giggled. Oh, God, she thought dolefully. She'd regressed to girlhood. It must be a recurring condition. One that affected her anytime Jeff Bradford was around.

Holding his free hand to his abused ribs with an exaggerated wince, Jeff kept his other arm around her shoulders as they left the arcade in unspoken consent. "How about some ice cream? I've been craving ice cream ever since Webb mentioned it earlier."

"Sounds good," Autumn agreed, matching her steps to his as they walked down the sidewalk. She wondered briefly how Webb's evening with Emily and Ryan had gone, then dismissed them from her mind. She was enjoying her own date with Jeff too much to concentrate on anyone else just then. She allowed her arm to slide around his waist, linking them as they strolled. Sometimes it was nice to feel like a schoolgirl, she reflected wryly.

"Chocolate mint for the lady," Jeff told the teenager behind the Christmas-decorated counter of the ice-cream store, smiling into Autumn's eyes as he spoke.

She returned the smile. "And cherry vanilla for the gentleman," she murmured, remembering their conversation from the restaurant the previous Saturday.

Grinning at the total self-absorption of the couple, the teenager obligingly scooped generous helpings of the ice cream into waffle cones. Jeff paid for the ice cream, then winked at the kid, who laughed and gave Jeff a thumbs-up gesture of approval.

"What was that all about?" Autumn demanded curiously as they left the store.

"Male bonding," Jeff answered flippantly, taking her hand to lead her off the sidewalk and onto the nearly deserted beach that stretched before them.

"You're all hopeless." Autumn sighed, curling her fingers around his as she licked her ice cream. She'd pulled Emily's red sweater over her head just before they'd gone into the ice-cream store, and now she was grateful for its light protection as a cool breeze blew moistly off the bay, catching strands of hair loosened from her banana clip and wafting them around her face. The predicted cold front had arrived, dropping the temperature to a cool—for Tampa—fifty degrees. The moon shone brightly in the clear early-December sky above them, and the waters of the bay glittered in its light. She couldn't remember ever seeing a more beautiful night—but then, she'd never spent a night like this with Jeff. Something told her that it wouldn't have seemed quite so perfect without him.

"Beautiful night," Jeff murmured, seeming to read her thoughts.

"Mmm. A lot different from Arkansas at this time of year."

"Is that right?" Jeff asked gravely, swiping his tongue over his ice cream.

Watching him, Autumn shivered, but the tremor had little to do with the weather. Swallowing hard, she nibbled at her ice cream and nodded. "I'll, uh, I'll have to pack warm clothing when I go home for Christmas in a couple of weeks. I've gotten spoiled by Florida winters, even though I've only been through one so far."

Jeff was watching her as she chattered, his eyes warmly amused. A dribble of cherry vanilla ice cream slid down one side of his cone, and he slowly licked it clean.

Autumn felt a moan forming in her chest and hastily repressed it. When had this happened? she wondered frantically. *How* had this happened? One minute they'd been laughing and playing, as comfortable together as kids, and in the next she found herself wanting to pull him to the damp sand and have her wicked way with him. *Bewitched.*

"How's your ice cream?" Jeff inquired, his voice a low rumble meant for her ears alone.

"It's . . . it's fine. How's yours?"

"Very good. Want a taste?"

"Um, no, thanks."

"Mind if I taste yours?"

"Go ahead." She held her cone out to him.

Ignoring it, he turned and lowered his mouth to hers, kissing her for the first time that evening. Autumn closed her eyes and clung to him with her free hand, feeling as if she were melting faster than the ice cream still clutched in her other hand. Chocolate mint and cherry vanilla combined in the most exotically erotic taste she'd ever experienced as Jeff deepened the kiss. "Mmm," he murmured when he finally released her mouth. "Delicious."

It took her a full minute to catch her breath. By that time Jeff had already turned her in the crook of his arm and begun to walk again. Spotting a trash can, Autumn tossed the remains of her ice-cream cone into it. It seemed to have lost its flavor. Without a word Jeff followed her example. She looked up to find him staring down at her. Her head tilted back, her eyelids closed, and he was kissing her again, thoroughly, hungrily, as if he'd been wanting to do so for hours, for days, for a week.

Jeff tightened his arms around her, his body hardening, his mind beginning to whirl. He'd long since accepted that kissing her had these effects on him; each time was more wondrous, more necessary than the last. He dimly realized that he'd held off kissing her earlier because he'd known he wouldn't want to stop when he did. The past week had been hell, wanting to be with her, wanting to hold her. The past few hours had been heaven, touching her, laughing with her.

Six weeks earlier he'd looked into emerald green eyes and fallen in love. Now he acknowledged that his love was real, lasting, deep. Forever. He'd found his mate, the other half of himself, and he would do whatever he had to do to make her his. Fight whatever battles were necessary. Even if Autumn herself were the opponent. And she would be.

Tearing his mouth from hers, he gasped for breath and buried his face in her throat. "I want you," he muttered. "I didn't know it was possible to want anyone this much."

"Shouldn't we go someplace more private?" Autumn asked softly, her voice a husky siren's lure.

"Yes," he whispered in response, raising his head to look down at her. He could read her desire for him in her eyes and he shuddered. She wanted him. She didn't love him—yet—but she wanted him. Maybe—just for tonight—that would be enough. Maybe.

They talked little during the drive. Jeff guided his silver BMW with one hand, keeping Autumn's hand in the other. Occasionally he raised her hand to brush her knuckles with his lips. By the time he pulled into her driveway, she was trembling with need for him.

She didn't have to ask him in. Without a word he opened his door and climbed out of the car, meeting her on the other side. She could feel the slight unsteadiness in his arm when it slipped around her waist, the hint of vulnerability increasing her own uncharacteristic shyness. It took her three tries to fit the key into the lock of her front door.

The door had barely closed behind them before she was in his arms again, his mouth slanting hungrily over hers. Rising on her tiptoes to press closer against him, Autumn abandoned herself wholly to sensation, shutting off all thought of consequences. She wanted him. And this time she was going to have him.

Jeff's first impulse was to lift her into his arms and carry her into the bedroom. A soft chuckle left his throat as he realized that his fiery love probably wouldn't appreciate such a gesture. She'd want to walk beside him, if not actually lead him.

Autumn tilted her head back to look up at him, her eyes quizzical. "You're laughing?" she inquired curiously, her voice disturbed.

"I'm happy," he answered simply, smiling down at her. He wanted so desperately to add that he loved her. But he couldn't. Not yet. His smile dimmed.

Autumn lifted a hand to his cheek, her own smile misty. "So am I," she told him softly. "It's been a wonderful evening."

He caught her hand in his fiercely, gripped by needs too powerful to control. He ached for her, the desire all too close to pain. He could lose himself in her, pretend that she was his for eternity. But, dammit, he didn't want to have to pretend. He wanted it to be true. "I need you," he whispered rawly, turning his face into her palm. "God, I need you."

As he'd known she would, she interpreted his words to mean that he wanted to make love with her. She could not—or would not—read the deeper meaning hidden within them. Her full red lips curving into a smile that no man could resist, she twined her fingers around his and turned to guide him to her bedroom.

She snapped on a small bedside lamp, illuminating the room with soft golden light. Jeff's eyes turned swiftly to examine her bedroom and what he saw made him smile. Like Autumn, her room was an intriguing combination of the defiantly modern and the sweetly old-fashioned. It was perfect for her. Just as she was perfect for him. He turned back to her in time to watch her sweep the borrowed red sweater over her head. Her sultry gaze holding his, she removed the clip from her hair, allowing the wind-tangled auburn tresses to fall around her shoulders. He swallowed hard.

No one else in the world would have known she was nervous as she reached for the top button of her blouse, Jeff thought in a sudden surge of fierce possessiveness. Surely no one else could have seen beyond that cool, seductive exterior to find the trace of uncertainty in her eyes, in the almost imperceptible tremor of her fingers as they loosened that button and then the next. He took the two steps that separated them and caught her hands in his, raising them tenderly to his lips. And then he finished unbuttoning her blouse, sliding the crisp fabric off her shoulders to expose full, creamy breasts spilling over the lacy top of a scrap of a bra. He groaned and lowered his lips to the tempting, gold-dusted flesh.

Autumn quivered when his mouth touched her skin. Glorying in her response, Jeff lowered her to the bed, following to stretch out beside her. Still without removing her bra, he cupped one swollen breast in his hand, his lips and teeth tracing the line of lace that covered her. "You're so beautiful. So very beautiful." He barely recognized his own voice.

"Jeff," she whispered, arching up to him.

His name on her lips was the most erotic sound he'd ever heard. He had to taste it. "My name," he muttered roughly. "Say it again."

"Jeff," she moaned as his fingers found her straining nipple through thin lace. "Je—"

And then his mouth was on hers, his tongue deep inside to claim the sound. Rolling to lie on top of her, he arched into her softness, the clothing between them unwanted barriers to total intimacy. Burying his hands deep in her hair, he kissed her with all the unleashed passion inside him, his control almost completely shattered. And she kissed him back with a heat that equaled his, her silky, work-strong arms going around him to clutch him to her. Her pant-clad legs tangled with his, the feminine juncture of her thighs willingly cradling his straining hardness.

"How do you do this to me, Autumn Reed?" he whispered between hot, stinging kisses. "What kind of a spell have you cast on me with those green sorceress eyes?"

Her laugh was thin, breathless. "And I thought I was the one who'd been bewitched," she accused him, her hands stroking the strong line of his back.

Holding her still beneath him, Jeff lifted his head and stared down at her. "Tell me you want me, Autumn. I need to hear it."

"I want you, Jeff," she answered without hesitation.

He groaned and kissed her again, his hand seeking the clasp of her bra. It was enough, he told himself thickly. It was enough—for now. It had to be.

And then he groaned again when a high-pitched beeping penetrated the thick fog of desire inside his head. Cursing beneath his breath, he forced himself to roll away from her, his hand going to the small plastic box clipped to his belt. "I'm sorry."

Her breathing as ragged as his, Autumn struggled upright, pushing her hair out of her face with an unsteady hand. "Don't apologize. It's not your fault."

Checking the telephone number displayed on the tiny screen of the pager, Jeff nodded toward the extension phone on her bedside table. "May I?"

"Of course." Autumn reached self-consciously for her blouse. *So this is what it's like to date a doctor,* she thought with an attempt at humor that she didn't at all feel.

She couldn't help hearing Jeff's end of the conversation as she buttoned her blouse. "What's up, Julian?" he asked, his voice still husky with passion. "She is? Tonight? Damn. I was hoping she'd make it through Christmas. No, I'm glad you called. I want to be with her mother when it happens. Hang around, will you? I'll be there soon. Thanks, Julian."

Running his hands through his tousled hair, Jeff turned to Autumn when he'd replaced the receiver, and there was sadness in his eyes. "I've got to go," he told her. "I'm losing a patient tonight, a little girl with cystic fibrosis. I want to be there for her mother."

"I understand. I'm sorry." She wanted to reach out to him, to ease the pain she read in him, but she didn't know how.

"I'm sorry, too. For everything." His awkward gesture at the rumpled bed said as much as his words.

Autumn shrugged, feeling her face grow hot. "I know."

Jeff started to turn toward the bedroom door, then he stopped suddenly, as if on impulse, and turned back to her. "Maybe it's best that this happened tonight. Before we made love."

Puzzled, she tilted her head to one side and looked up at him. "Why?"

Again he ran his hand through his hair, an atypically nervous gesture from him. "Because I'm not sure I could ever walk away from you if we make love," he blurted out at length. "Because once we've taken that step, I couldn't bear the thought of another man being with you, touching you. Hell, I can't bear that thought now. It's already too late for me. But you've been given a reprieve, Autumn. Another chance."

"Another chance for what?" she asked warily, moistening suddenly dry lips.

Moving abruptly, he cradled her face in both his hands, gently forcing her to look up at him. "Another chance to back away from the relationship developing between us before we lose control of it. I'm not talking about sex, Autumn. I won't deny that I want you, that I want to make love to you more than I've ever wanted another woman, but that's only a part of what I feel for you. I want a future, a commitment. And making love with you will only strengthen those feelings."

Her heart pounded in her chest, her hands trembled, and she recognized the symptoms of pure fear. This was what she'd tried to avoid from the beginning. Somehow she'd known that Jeff wouldn't meekly participate in the no-strings-attached affair she'd tried to convince herself she wanted with him. "Then maybe we'd better end it, Jeff. Because I'm *not* looking for a commitment right now. Believe me, it wouldn't work. I'm not the right woman for you. For an affair, maybe, some good times. But not for anything more lasting."

"You're wrong," he told her, his eyes blazing. "You're exactly the right woman for me. I've known from the moment I saw you. And don't try to convince me that you make a habit of indulging in a string of affairs. I won't believe you."

She lifted her chin in an instinctively defensive gesture at his too-close accusation. "You don't know that. You couldn't know."

"I know," he answered simply.

She jerked away from him, stepping back to put space between them. "Hadn't you better go to the hospital?"

"Yes. I wish I could stay so we could talk about this some more, but I can't. I'll call you tomorrow."

"No," she said quickly. "Don't."

"Autumn..."

"Please, Jeff. I need time. I'm not ready for this now."

He sighed and nodded. "All right. I shouldn't have brought up my feelings like this, knowing I didn't have time to stay and talk it out. But I didn't want to leave you thinking that all I want from you is an affair."

He closed the distance between them again and dropped a brief kiss on her still-swollen lips. "Think about us, Autumn. Think about the feelings that have been there between us from the beginning. More than passion, more than desire. Don't be afraid of those feelings, honey."

Honey. She'd always disliked that endearment, considered it demeaning. So why did the word make her knees go weak when spoken so softly by Jeff? "I..." She what? Wordlessly she stared at him.

"It's your move again, Autumn. I'll be waiting when you're ready to make it. Good night." He turned and moved away from her, his long strides quickly crossing the living room to the front door.

Some impulse made her run after him. "Jeff!"

He paused, holding the door open. "What is it, Autumn?"

Stopping only inches from him, she touched his cheek fleetingly. "I'm very sorry about the little girl. I know it hurts you."

He caught her hand and pressed a warm kiss into her palm. "Thank you," he whispered roughly. "Good night, Autumn."

"Good night, Jeff."

"Damn. Damn, damn, damn." Autumn dropped onto the couch and buried her face in hands. She'd known. She'd *known* to stay away from him! And it was her own fault that she hadn't. She'd called *him* for that first date.

From the beginning she'd known the kind of man he was. Warm, sensitive, honorable. Modern in some ways, but not when it came to relationships. The man wanted a wife, a family, and now he'd decided Autumn was the woman he'd been looking for.

He was so very wrong.

Her eyes stung with hot tears she refused to shed. She didn't want to hurt Jeff. She didn't want to be hurt. Yet both seemed inevitable now. How could she have deluded herself into thinking there was any other possible ending to this thing between them?

He needed someone to cherish, someone to protect. She needed to take care of herself. He would be the kind of man to love with his entire heart, to center his life on that love. She was terrified of being smothered by that type of love. He needed someone to be there for him when he hurt, someone to come home to when he'd lost one of the patients he cared so deeply about. She didn't know how to offer that kind of support. She couldn't even help him tonight when she could see him suffering in front of her. Dammit, she didn't know how!

A damp, cold nose pressed against her cheek, and Autumn automatically gathered the small white dog into her arms. "Oh, Babs, I've made such a mess of everything," she whispered sadly. "Such a terrible mess."

LONG HOURS LATER Jeff stepped out of his shower and rubbed a towel over his dripping hair. A weary sigh escaped him as he walked nude to his bed after patting most of the water from his body. He was so damn tired. He crawled into the bed and stretched out on his stomach, one arm draped around his pillow. He desperately needed sleep, but it was slow in coming. Part of his mind was still at the hospital, with the little girl who'd died and the family whose grief was so devastating despite the efforts they'd made to prepare themselves for this inevitable event. Yet another part of his mind was with Autumn, hoping that he hadn't ruined everything with the impulsive declaration of his feelings.

He didn't regret telling her that he wanted more from her than an affair. He'd never intended to pretend differently. He only hoped he hadn't frightened her away with the ill-timed admission.

Drawing in a long, ragged breath, he burrowed more deeply into the pillow and allowed himself to drift into a pleasant fantasy in which Autumn was lying beside him, her fingers stroking his hair, her skin pressed warmly to his. The merest hint of a smile touched his lips at the thought. Someday, he promised himself as consciousness slipped away from him, someday it would happen. Surely he couldn't need her this much and never be allowed to have her.

AUTUMN SPENT the next two weeks working until she was nearly exhausted in an attempt to convince herself that she didn't miss Jeff, didn't think of him every waking moment. She succeeded only in losing five pounds she hadn't tried to lose and developing purple circles under her eyes from too many restless nights. As she'd requested, Jeff didn't call, but she knew that he was waiting for her to call him. A dozen times she found herself standing with her hand on the telephone. She would always stop herself at the last moment from calling him, remembering the intensity in his voice when he'd told her that he wanted more from her than an affair.

She welcomed the beginning of her Christmas vacation. She had planned to leave Babs in a kennel during her visit to Arkansas, but Emily insisted on keeping the dog. Since Babs knew and liked both Emily and Ryan, Autumn was comfortable with the arrangement, and she left Tampa with a sense of optimism. Surely it would be easier not to think of Jeff when several hundred miles separated them, she thought as she boarded the plane for Little Rock Regional Airport. She hoped to return to Tampa in two weeks completely cured of her infatuation for one nearly irresistible doctor.

She arrived in Little Rock just after noon on Friday, the week before Christmas, expecting Spring to meet her at the airport as they'd arranged. Instead, she was met by a veritable welcoming committee—Spring, Clay, Summer and Derek. Laughing happily, the three sisters exchanged fervent hugs, all trying to talk at once.

"What are you all doing here?"

"We came to meet you, Sis. What else?" Summer replied cheerfully, her brilliant blue eyes dancing with mischief beneath her fringe of honey-brown bangs. "Derek and I arrived yesterday and we spent the night at Spring and Clay's house. We thought we'd all drive to Rose Bud together this afternoon. Spring's closed her office for the rest of the day, and she and Clay can spend the whole weekend with the rest of us in Rose Bud, though she has to work Monday."

"But I'll be back in Rose Bud on the evening of the twenty-third," Spring put in, a smile in the violet eyes that regarded Autumn through light-framed glasses. "Clay and I have both announced that we're closing our offices from the twenty-fourth through the twenty-sixth, so we'll have those three days to spend together, too."

"This is great," Autumn enthused. "Summer, I'm so glad you could make it home this year. We missed you last year."

"Derek made sure that nothing kept us away this year. Poor thing's worked himself half to death during the past few weeks to arrange it."

Autumn smiled at the man behind Summer, eyeing his lean yet muscular six-foot frame and dark tan. "You look pretty healthy to me, Derek."

Derek Anderson smiled in return, leaning over to kiss her cheek. "You know how Summer exaggerates."

"My turn," another male voice insisted, and then Autumn found herself caught in a hearty embrace and thoroughly kissed.

"Hi, Clay," she managed to say when he released her amid the laughter of the others. "I see you haven't changed a bit."

"Nope," the six-four, sinfully handsome blonde replied cheerfully. "Why try to alter perfection?"

Spring groaned and rolled her eyes at her husband's immodest quip.

"It'll take us a little over an hour to get to Rose Bud," Clay mused, glancing at his colorful Swatch watch. Then he grinned boyishly at Autumn as they walked toward the parking lot. "That'll give you plenty of time to tell us all about the new man in your life."

Autumn stopped in her tracks, appalled to feel herself blushing—again, dammit. As the others stared at her, she realized that it was the first time her sisters had seen her blush in years. "What..." She stopped and cleared her throat, glaring at Clay. "What new man?"

"The one who can make you blush," Summer added avidly, taking her sister's arm. "Okay, Autumn, who is he?"

Groaning, Autumn allowed herself to be hustled along, though she was determined to change the subject the minute the five of them were settled in Spring's car. She had no intention of discussing Jeff Bradford with two happily married couples!

Were her confused feelings for him really so obvious that her family had noticed a change in her that quickly? she wondered ruefully. Maybe it wouldn't be quite so easy to put him out of her mind during the next two weeks after all.

7

"ARE YOU SURE you're warm enough, Spring? Do you want me to bring your sweater?"

"No, thank you, Clay, I'm fine."

"Well, how about something to eat? D'you want a sandwich or something? You have to keep up your strength."

"Clay!" Spring protested, making Autumn smile at the exasperated look on her older sister's face. "Isn't Gil waiting for you?"

Clay bit his lower lip thoughtfully. "Yeah, he is, but I can stay home if you need me. I don't have to watch football with Gil."

"Please go," Spring said firmly. "This is my last chance to visit with Autumn before she returns to Florida, and you promised Gil and me that you'd spend a couple of hours with him. Now go."

"Don't worry, Clay, I'll take care of her," Autumn promised gravely, trying not to laugh. She was spending New Year's Day, the last day of her vacation in Arkansas, at Spring and Clay's lovely nearly renovated older Victorian home in Little Rock. Clay would drive her to the airport the next morning to catch her flight back to Tampa. She'd enjoyed her visit very much, but she was ready to go home. She tried to tell herself that Babs and her job were the main reasons she was in such a hurry to get back.

Clay looked sheepish but smiled at Autumn in gratitude. "Thanks. You know where I can be reached if you need me." He leaned over to give his wife a long, passionate kiss before allowing himself to be shooed out of the room.

The sisters waited until the front door had closed behind him and the sound of his car engine had faded before giving in to the gales of laughter they'd been holding back. Reclining comfortably on her couch, her dainty yellow-and-white cat curled in her lap, Spring rolled her eyes in mock dismay. "Seven more months of this! Maybe I shouldn't have told him about the baby until closer to the due date."

"Spring, I think he would have noticed," Autumn remarked dryly, swinging her foot in front of her as she lounged in a large wing chair.

"It seemed like such a nice idea to tell him on Christmas Eve—kind of like an extra Christmas present. I should have known that he would overreact."

"Oh, I don't know. I think he's kind of sweet. I particularly liked it when he refused to allow you to open your own presents in case you got a paper cut or something."

Spring groaned and buried her face in her hands. "Oh, God. I'll never survive this pregnancy."

Pregnancy. Autumn shook her head slowly, trying to comprehend the reality of the word. In just seven short months Spring would be a mother. Autumn would be an aunt. Her parents would be grandparents. It was mind-boggling, thinking of the new generation beginning in her family.

Spring had made her announcement to the family on Christmas Day, to the general delight of the Reed clan. It had been a wonderful holiday, and Autumn had enjoyed being with her family again. She'd been a bit concerned that, as the only sister left unmarried, her family would show an even greater tendency than usual to treat her as the "baby," something that had always frustrated Autumn. Yet, for the first time, she felt this year that she'd been treated as an adult, a capable, intelligent career woman.

Maybe it was because she'd been on her own for several years now, or maybe because the two newest family members, Derek and Clay, had never known her as the "cute little tomboy" and therefore didn't treat her as such. Whatever the reason, Autumn was grateful. Though various members of the family had commented that Autumn seemed to have changed in some way since her last visit home, Autumn had managed to change the subject each time. She was fully aware that she had displayed an uncharacteristic tendency to drift off into her thoughts during her holiday, particularly since Spring had made her announcement. She was also aware that, rather than putting Jeff out of her mind on this vacation away from him, he was as much a part of her thoughts as before.

Autumn had been reexamining her goals in life during the past two weeks, finding contradictions within herself that she hadn't realized were there. Until she'd met Jeff, she'd thought she wanted nothing more out of life than a fulfilling career, a company of her own that would bring her financial security and a satisfying degree of responsibility. When she'd thought of marriage at all, it had been as a nebulous possibility, perhaps when she was fully established, well into her thirties.

Now she found herself wondering what it would be like to be married, sharing her life with a man full-time. Wondering if a mother who drove a pickup truck and strapped on a tool pouch could make a nice home for a dark-haired, blue-eyed child. No, she wouldn't allow herself to get that specific in her wondering. This was strictly hypothetical curiosity on her part.

"Aren't you terrified?" The words left her mouth without conscious thought.

Spring looked a bit surprised for a moment, then smiled understandingly at the younger sister who'd always been so intense about life's roles and responsibilities. "I guess I am, a little," she admitted. "It's not like the baby's going to arrive with an owner's manual. Like any first-time mother, I'll be playing it by ear a lot. But I already love this baby so much. And Clay will be a wonderful father."

"What about your career? Will you be able to dedicate as much time and energy to your practice after the baby arrives?"

"I'll certainly have to make some changes, and I haven't worked them all out yet. I don't know how long I'll be able to take off for maternity leave, for example. I'll have to work with my patients as much as possible so they won't be forced to go elsewhere. Fortunately, there aren't that many emergencies in optometry, so we should be able to work around the four to six weeks that I'm off."

"And after the baby's born?"

"I'll start talking to other working mothers soon about the different types of child care available in the area. I know attorneys, retailers, bankers and doctors who also happen to be mothers. Good mothers. I'm sure they'll be more than happy to offer advice. My baby will be well cared for, Autumn."

Autumn smiled. "You don't have to convince me of that. I happen to think my niece or nephew is very lucky to have you and Clay for parents."

"Thanks."

Autumn twisted a curl of auburn hair around one finger, wondering how to word her next question, but feeling the need to ask. "Isn't it driving you crazy? The way you're being treated now, I mean? Like you've suddenly become a delicate, emotional creature that people have to tiptoe around. Mother hovered over you, Daddy kept patting your cheek, and Clay—Lord!"

Spring laughed. "Yes, it drives me crazy. But I guess that's just part of it. I understand that, as I get bigger, all people will focus on is my belly. My attorney friend said it was terribly frustrating when the jury kept smiling at her stomach instead of frowning thoughtfully into her eyes as she wanted them to do. She had to work twice as hard to be taken seriously while she was pregnant. No one ever said it was going to be easy, Autumn. But becoming an optometrist wasn't easy, either. I had to work for it. It was worth it.

"As for Clay... well, he's just Clay. Part of his solicitude is teasing, the other part is his way of being involved in a phase of parenthood during which the father has very little to do. Fathers feel terribly left out during pregnancy. I plan to keep him very busy for the next seven months."

Suddenly restless, Autumn sprang to her feet and began to pace around the impeccably decorated room. "You and Summer make it look so easy. You have careers, goals, plans—and yet you still make time for your husbands and look forward to having children. How do you do it?"

"Autumn, it's not easy. It's not. But it's what we want."

"But how do you *know*?" Autumn turned to look at her sister, the frustration building inside her as she tried to understand the other woman's serenity. "Neither you nor Summer seemed all that anxious to get married before you met Clay and Derek. You were busy with your practice, and Summer was having too much fun partying with her nutty San Francisco friends to care about settling down. Then you meet these guys, and suddenly you're buying homes and making babies. Was it really that simple?"

"Simple?" Spring repeated incredulously, her eyes widening. "Autumn, it was terrifying! You've heard us talk about how insecure and uncertain we were in the early stages of our romances."

She paused for a moment, her expression dreamy with her memories, then she smiled at her intently listening sister. "It wasn't simple, Autumn. I don't think it's ever simple to suddenly have another person become such an important part of your life. I only know that I feel so fulfilled now. I'm still my own person with my own goals and career, but I always have Clay when I need someone to share my thoughts and dreams and disappointments, and he has me for the same type of moral support."

She shot Autumn a sly glance, turning the conversation abruptly in a new direction. "I think that you would thrive within a happy marriage, just as Summer and I have. Maybe it's the way we were raised, with our parents setting such a good example of two people whose lives are better for being shared with the ones they love."

Autumn swallowed and started to pace again. "We weren't talking about me," she said gruffly.

"Weren't we?" Spring inquired gently. "Then why is it suddenly so important for you to understand how Summer and I justified marriage?"

Autumn moistened her lips and avoided her sister's knowing eyes. "I was just curious."

"Want to tell me about him?"

"About who?"

"The man Clay asked you about the day you arrived, the man who made you blush," Spring teased. "The man who has you asking yourself if marriage is such a terrible thing after all."

"That's ridiculous," Autumn blustered, her arms crossing defensively over her chest. "You know how I feel about marriage. I came close once, remember? I thought I was in love with Steven, but I couldn't marry him. Just the thought made me panic."

"You *thought* you were in love with Steven," Spring repeated. "You weren't. You were infatuated with his good looks and football-hero image. And you were much too young five years ago to be thinking about marriage. You've made a life for yourself now, accomplished things that you couldn't have done if you'd married then. That doesn't mean you couldn't have it all now." She paused for only a moment before asking again, "So want to tell me about this new man?"

"There's nothing to tell," Autumn answered, then had to be honest. "Well, not much. I've only known him for a couple of months, and we've only had two dates. But he's... He makes me... He... Oh, hell, Spring, I don't know. I seem to be obsessed with the man, but I don't know if it's something serious or if it's just a bad case of lust."

Spring laughed delightedly. "Oh, does this sound familiar!"

"So what am I supposed to do?" Autumn demanded, shoving her hands into the pockets of her jeans and glaring at her amused sister. "Jeff's a very traditional kind of man. One who's looking for permanence, commitment. I don't know if that's what I want. What if it isn't?"

"What if it is?" Spring asked in return. "How will you know unless you give it a chance?"

"I don't want to hurt him. And I don't want to be hurt," Autumn murmured, finally putting into words the fears that had plagued her for the past few weeks.

"There's always that risk," Spring agreed. "But you've never been a coward, Autumn. Far from it. You've always willingly taken on every challenge that faced you. I can't give you advice because I don't know Jeff or anything about him, but I do believe that you can accomplish anything you set your mind to—a career, a marriage, a family. I always knew that when you fell in love, you'd fall hard. You've never done anything halfway."

In love? Was she in love with Jeff? Autumn frowned, going cold at the suggestion. Was this how her sisters had felt? If so, then "terrified" seemed suddenly too tame a word. Autumn was scared spitless.

Spring set Missy, her cat, onto the floor and rose to her feet, assuming the stance of a concerned older sister. "Would I approve of Jeff, Autumn?"

With a reluctant laugh Autumn grimaced. "You'd adore him. He's almost too handsome to be real, he loves kids and animals, his manners are straight out of an old handbook for Southern gentlemen, and yet he's modern enough to clean up after himself and not be threatened when a woman asks him out. I think he'd be a bit overprotective of the woman in his life, but he doesn't seem to be bothered by the idea of being involved with a working woman. And he's got a smile that could melt granite."

Intrigued, Spring straightened her glasses and peered thoughtfully at her sister. "What does he do?"

"He's a pediatrician."

"Marry the man."

Autumn laughed at Spring's flat statement. "I should have known that's what you'd say."

"I'm not kidding. He sounds perfect!"

"Not perfect, but damn close." Autumn ran her fingers through her hair and winced. "And that's what scares the hell out of me. I think he deserves a whole lot more than what I can give him."

"You *are* in love!" Spring exclaimed. "You're worried about whether you're good enough for him! Believe me, Autumn, you are. He'd be lucky to have you."

"And *you're* just a bit prejudiced," Autumn answered fondly. "You're family."

"True. And I love you. I'll bet Jeff does, too. I can't wait to meet him."

"Could we talk about something else for a while?" Autumn asked weakly. "This conversation is making me nervous."

Spring chuckled. "Come into my room, Sis. I've got something to give you."

Curious, Autumn followed her sister from the room, still uncertain about her feelings for Jeff but somehow comforted by having shared her concerns with Spring.

"STOP LOOKING AT ME like that, Babs. I told you I missed you. Believe me, you wouldn't have enjoyed

Arkansas this time. You'd have frozen your fuzzy little tail off." Autumn kept up a running conversation with the dog tagging at her heels as she unpacked, neatly putting away her clothing and Christmas presents. "Besides, Emily told me that you had a great time visiting her and Ryan. I'll bet you're spoiled rotten now."

Closing the last drawer of her bedroom chest, she stretched and looked contentedly around the room. It was good to be home. She chuckled as she glanced at the pillows of her bed, where a large, ragged stuffed bear reclined regally, appearing quite pleased with himself, although his orange fur was a bit mangy-looking and he was missing one ear. Winnie the Pooh had been the "something" that Spring had given Autumn the day before after their conversation about Jeff. The bear had belonged to Spring as a child, then had been passed down to Summer and Autumn in turn. Autumn had been quite attached to the bear, dragging him around for years by the now-missing ear. On a whim, she'd given the stuffed toy to Summer when Summer had moved to San Francisco. Summer had declared her intention of moving to a city where she knew absolutely no one as a means of recovering her self-sufficiency after her accident, and Autumn sent Pooh along to keep her sister company.

Spring had received the bear at the end of her twelve-day visit to California in March. Knowing that Spring was leaving with a broken heart after a quarrel with Clay, Summer had impulsively sent Pooh home with her older sister. And now Spring had completed the cycle again, returning the old toy to the youngest Reed sister.

"I think he brings good luck," Spring had said gravely, though her violet eyes had sparkled with amusement at the whimsical ceremony. "And he makes a great confidant."

The gesture had appealed to Autumn's sense of humor, and she'd obligingly brought the bear home with her. Besides, she thought, patting the worn fuzzy head, she'd missed old Pooh. Babs tended to get restless if squeezed too tightly, though she was definitely the better conversationalist.

Smiling to herself, Autumn realized that her visit home had been good for her. She had her sense of humor back, she was well rested and she had finally come to a decision about Jeff. She was going to make the move that he was waiting for her to make. She'd never be comfortable leaving the situation between them unresolved. Keeping some distance between them for a few weeks had put her attraction for him back in perspective, she thought confidently. He was handsome, entertaining, amusing. There was no reason at all for her to avoid him when both of them wanted to be together—for now.

She glanced at the telephone, then quickly decided to wait a few hours before calling him. "Coward," she accused herself under her breath as she wandered into her kitchen to see if there was anything in the cabinets that she could have for dinner.

She had just closed the door to her discouragingly empty refrigerator—she'd cleaned it out before leaving—when her doorbell chimed.

"Jeff!" She really hadn't expected to find him on her doorstep. The last she'd heard, it had been her move. And suddenly she wasn't sure she was ready to make it. Oh, God, he looked wonderful, she thought on a silent wail. All her brave resolutions about keeping her attraction to him in perspective shattered into mental fragments, leaving her defenseless against him. All she could do was look at him, so tall and tanned and strong in the porch light, and fight the urge to throw herself into his arms and beg him to make love with her.

"Hi." Jeff turned one of his heart-stopping smiles on her, his eyes just a bit wary as they watched her so intently. His hands were in the pockets of the denim jacket he wore with a white Oxford shirt and jeans, his feet spread apart as if he were prepared for anything. She wondered if he were that uncertain of his reception. "I know I should have called first, but when I drove by and saw your lights on, I couldn't resist stopping."

"Come in, Jeff," Autumn invited him, moving back to give him room to pass her. She glanced down quickly at her own green sweater and gray slacks, relieved to see that they had traveled well. She resisted the impulse to lift a hand to her hair, knowing that her French braid was still quite neat. "You, uh, you just happened to be passing by?" she asked skeptically, leaning back against the door.

His mouth twisted into a self-mocking smile. "Every day for the past week," he answered quietly. "I wasn't sure when you'd be back." He paused for a moment, then added, "I missed you, Autumn."

"I, uh . . ." She swallowed. "Sit down, Jeff. Can I get you anything? I haven't been to the grocery store yet, but I can make coffee."

"No, thanks." Still watching her closely, he took a step toward her and then another, until he stood only inches away from her. "Did you have a nice vacation?"

"Yes." Her voice was little more than a whisper as her body reacted to his proximity by jumping into overdrive, heart pounding, breath quickening, palms dampening. She tried to keep the conversation polite and unthreatening, though she felt as if she were fighting a losing battle. "Did you enjoy the holidays?"

Jeff lifted a hand to her face, fingertips tracing the line of her jaw from ear to chin. "As much as possible without having you with me," he replied softly, so close now that she could almost feel his breath on her flushed skin. "I thought of you constantly. I wanted you with me at Christmas, singing carols and opening presents. And I wanted to kiss you at midnight to welcome in the New Year. Did you think of me while you were gone, Autumn?"

She was unable to answer with less than complete honesty. "I thought of you. A lot."

He raised his other hand so that her face was cupped tenderly within his palms. "And?" he prompted.

"And I missed you." She sighed, her gaze locked with his. "I didn't come to any great decision about us, Jeff. I'm still not ready to make promises or commitments, but I know that I don't want to stop seeing you. Not yet."

A flicker of emotion in his eyes told her that he wasn't quite satisfied with her answer, but he suppressed it almost immediately. He touched his lips to her forehead. "I guess that'll have to do for now. It's enough—almost—that you did miss me during these past few weeks. They've been the longest weeks of my life, Autumn. I told you I'd let you make the next move, but I couldn't stay away any longer."

"I did miss you, Jeff." She let her hands go hesitantly to his waist, then creep around to stroke his back. "I would have called you tonight. I wanted to see you."

"I'm glad." His lips moved downward, touching the tip of her nose before hovering over her mouth. "I've been saving this kiss for forty-three hours. Happy New Year, Autumn."

He gave her no opportunity to respond verbally. His mouth slanted over hers with a hunger that overwhelmed her, drawing an immediate and equal response from her. His arms tightened around her, pulling her hard against him. Her own arms went up to circle his neck, fitting them perfectly together. So perfectly that she felt bereft when at length he released her mouth and stepped backward to put a few inches between them.

"Have you eaten?" he asked.

She honestly couldn't remember for a moment. Then she shook her head. "No. Not since lunch."

"Have dinner with me?"

"Yes." And anything else he wanted, she told him with her eyes.

He caught his breath and looked quickly down at his shoes, forcibly clearing his throat. "I..." He paused, then started again. "I almost forgot. I brought you a Christmas present." He reached inside his denim jacket.

Autumn watched him with a smile, finding his momentary uncertainty rather endearing. "I don't have one for you."

"Don't you?" He gave her a quick grin, then held out two thin cardboard rectangles.

Curious, Autumn looked down at the tickets he pressed into her hand. "Jeremy Kane!" she said with a delighted gasp. "He's performing in St. Petersburg next month? I didn't even know."

"The tickets don't go on sale until Monday," Jeff informed her a bit smugly. "I pulled a few strings. You'll notice I gave you two of them. You can take anyone you like with you, but don't forget who made the effort to get them for you."

Autumn laughed, knowing he fully intended for one of the tickets to be used by him. Even as her laughter faded, she wondered if they would still be seeing each other when the popular magician made his appearance in seven more weeks. Jeff obviously thought they would be. Still, it had been incredibly nice of him to go to so much trouble to get her tickets to the performance that would certainly be a sellout, simply because she'd once mentioned that she wanted to see Jeremy Kane in person.

"Thank you, Jeff," she told him. For the first time since she'd known him, she made a completely spontaneous gesture toward him, rising on her tiptoes to place a lingering kiss on his beautifully shaped mouth.

Jeff's response was instantaneous, recently banked fires flaming again at her touch. The softness in her face just before she'd lifted her lips to his had proved his undoing. He'd thought he'd be able to restrain himself until after dinner at least, but he was shaken by a wave of desire that shattered any control he had managed to retain earlier. There had been no other woman for him since he'd first set eyes on Autumn just over two months before—for some months before that, actually—and he had wanted to make love to her from that very first moment. He'd told himself before that desire wasn't enough. He still wanted more—much more—from her, but he loved her so much that he couldn't wait any longer. Couldn't find the strength to resist what she was so sweetly offering.

"Autumn," he moaned into her mouth, "I want you so much. I don't think I can walk away from you this time."

"Good," she whispered in return, her arms going around him. "I don't think I can let you walk away this time."

He hesitated only a moment before sweeping her off her feet and into his arms, turning rapidly for her bedroom.

Momentarily startled, Autumn glanced up at him with a fleeting frown. "You do understand that I'm quite capable of making this walk on my own?"

"Yes." He smiled down at her without slowing his long, smooth strides.

She sighed and relaxed, allowing herself to luxuriate in his strength. "Just so you know," she murmured, snuggling into his shoulder.

He held her more tightly, blinking rapidly at the trusting gesture. He was in danger of worshiping this woman in his arms, he thought as he lowered her tenderly to her bed. He loved her when she was prickly and defensive and independent, he adored her when she was sweet and responsive and passionate. And yet, knowing how much of him she already possessed, he could only offer more of himself. His heart, his soul, his future. Whatever she would take.

"How do you get more beautiful each time I see you?" he asked softly, his hands going to her hair to loosen the intricate braid. Fascinated by the soft, dark red curls he set free, he threaded his fingers through the thick mass and then buried his face in it. "Ah, Autumn, you feel so good."

"So do you," she whispered, her hands sliding slowly down his back, palms flattened against the rough denim of his jacket. "But you have on so many clothes."

The sound he made was half laugh, half moan. He shrugged out of the jacket, tossing it to the floor before pulling his shirt over his head. He never took his eyes from her as his hands went to the buckle of his leather belt, nor did she look away. Instead, she lay still, her approval of the body being revealed to her evident on her face. He loved knowing that she found him attractive. He planned to demonstrate quite thoroughly how beautiful she was to him.

Only when his own clothes were lying in a careless heap on her rug did he reach for the hem of her soft green sweater. Moments later the sweater, her gray slacks and her lacy undergarments had joined his things on the floor, and finally they were as he'd longed for them to be. Skin to skin. Heart to heart. As close as a man and woman could be—almost. He held off from that final joining, determined that she would need to have him inside her as desperately as he needed to be there by the time he entered her.

He wanted to make their lovemaking perfect for her. And that included making sure there would be no unplanned consequences. "Autumn, if you're not protected, I can—"

"No, it's okay," she assured him huskily, not bothering to mention that she'd given in to the inevitable and visited her gynecologist soon after meeting Jeff.

Her breasts were full and straining when he cupped them in his hands. Her skin was soft, moist, lightly dusted with golden freckles. He reveled in the feel of it, the scent of it, the taste of it. Her rosy nipples pouted for his attention, and he flicked them with the tip of his tongue, causing her to gasp and arch upward. She cried out softly, burying her hands in his hair when he opened his mouth to draw her deeply inside.

Her stomach was flat, taut, quivering. He caressed the silken slope, his palm sliding downward, tactually memorizing every inch of her. The auburn curls below were crisp, springy, guarding her deepest, softest, most vulnerable part. He intimately explored the hidden folds as he continued to pleasure her breasts with his lips and tongue. He was hanging on to his control by the weakest of threads, his entire body throbbing, clamoring for release. Still he lingered, trembling with need, drawing out the pleasure-pain for as long as humanly possible.

"Jeff. I need you now," Autumn breathed raggedly, her hips arching into his touch. "I want you so much it hurts."

"I know, darling. Believe me, I know." His mouth took hers, tongue thrusting inside to join hers in a wild dance even as his fingers probed deeper. Autumn shuddered and writhed beneath him, her hands moving demandingly over him, no longer content to let him guide their pace. When she took him in her hand, her fingers sliding boldly over pulsing, swollen flesh, his tenuous control snapped.

"Oh, Jeff, *yes!*" she cried when he settled forcefully between her welcoming legs. And then she was arching upward, taking him deep inside, and all rational thought fled, leaving him lost in a maelstrom of sensation. Feelings too intense, too new to be described by words. Harsh breathing and hoarse murmurings. Not knowing whether the strangled sounds came from him or her or both of them.

And then she was shivering beneath him, her release triggering his, and Jeff thought he'd die from pure pleasure. Surely no man could experience such shattering joy and live.

I love you. I love you. Dear God, I love you. The words echoed over and over in his mind as he slipped into an oblivious gray aftermath, not caring whether he'd said them aloud or only in his thoughts. *I love you.*

8

IT WAS A VERY LONG TIME before Autumn summoned the strength to move. Jeff was lying beside her, his eyes closed, one arm draped across her breasts, but she knew that he was awake. Like her, he was making a very slow recovery from their lovemaking.

There were no words to describe what had happened between them. Nothing in her experience, not even in her fantasies, had prepared her. She would not have believed herself capable of losing control so completely, of being so thoroughly mesmerized by another person. It was as if their minds, as well as their bodies, had been joined, so that there was no separation between them. She would never have allowed anyone else that much power over her.

No, that sounded as if she'd had some choice in the matter. She hadn't. Jeff had touched her, and she'd lost herself in him. That simply.

Swallowing hard, she glanced swiftly around the deeply shadowed bedroom, illuminated only by the light spilling in from the living room. Everything looked the same. Bemused, she realized that the world had literally fallen away while Jeff had loved her. She had truly lost all sense of time and place and identity. Nothing had existed for her but him. The realization was daunting.

Jeff stirred at her side, and her gaze returned to him. A swath of light fell over him from the open doorway, creating interesting highlights and shadows on his golden skin. He was truly a beautiful man. Shoulders wide, buttocks tight, legs taut and long. Though he was lying on his stomach, she could clearly picture his chest, broad and tanned, lightly furred, angling down to a flat stomach and hard thighs. The rest of him was impressively proportioned, as well. To her utter amazement, her pulse quickened as the memories assailed her. Moments before she'd been exhaustedly satiated. How could she want him again so soon?

Jeff's dark eyelashes fluttered, then lifted. "Hi," he murmured as their gazes met.

"Hi."

"Are you okay?"

She smiled. "I'm fine."

He shifted his weight, settling himself more comfortably beside her, then lifted an eyebrow and reached behind him. They'd been so impatient that they hadn't even stopped to turn back the bedspread but had made love diagonally on the bed. Now he chuckled as he pulled the stuffed toy from beneath his shoulder. "Who's this?"

"That's Pooh. An old friend," she answered lightly, brushing a lock of dark hair away from his forehead, enjoying the intimacy of the gesture.

"A teddy bear? I hadn't expected such frivolity from you, Autumn."

Lifting her head in mock indignation, she scowled at him. "I'll have you to know that I'm as capable of frivolity as anyone. Besides, it's not a teddy bear. It's Winnie the Pooh."

"You do realize that he's missing an ear?"

"Mmm. I'm afraid I'm responsible for that."

"How'd you do it?"

"Summer tried to take him away from me once when she was five and I was four. I had a good grip on his ear, but she had the rest of him."

Jeff chuckled. "I can imagine you as a willful little girl, fighting with your sisters. You must have been adorable."

"I was a holy terror. It's a wonder I survived."

He pulled her head onto his shoulder and wrapped his arms around her. "You turned out quite nicely."

"Thank you. I'll bet you were a well-behaved little boy. Nice manners, clean clothes, an apple for teacher."

"Are you daring to call me perfect again?"

"Would I do that?"

"You would," he answered sternly. "As a matter of fact, I *was* a well behaved little boy."

"I knew it."

"Unless I lost my temper," he continued, ignoring her comment.

"You don't have a temper."

He laughed. "I'm afraid there are those who would gladly contradict you. I'll admit that I don't lose my temper very often, but when I do, I have a hard time controlling it. I'm not at all proud of that fact, you understand."

"You don't sound particularly ashamed of it, either."

"Only because you seem to like me better with flaws."

"I explained that. I start feeling insecure when you seem too perfect. But I think I can accept you with a temper and a soap-opera addiction."

His arms tightened fractionally around her bare shoulders. "If not, I'll gladly come up with some more vices." He sounded just a bit too serious to be entirely teasing.

Autumn quickly changed the subject. "Didn't I hear you mention dinner earlier this evening?"

Jeff went still, then laughed contritely. "Oh, honey, I'm sorry. You must be starved. It completely slipped my mind."

He'd called her "honey" again. She really should mention to him that she didn't like being called "honey." Or at least she hadn't liked it until she'd heard it said in his deep voice.

"Why don't we order a pizza?" she suggested, reluctant to go out again that evening.

"Good idea. Make it a large one with everything. My treat."

"No, mine. It was my idea, after all."

"I asked you for dinner, remember? It was my fault that we got distracted before we could eat."

"I had something to do with that distraction. And I—"

Jeff laughed and tugged her head to his to silence her with a kiss. "Forget it. You can buy the pizza. But next time I'm buying. Deal?"

"Deal." She grinned at him, well aware, as he was, that she hadn't cared less who paid for the pizza. She just liked arguing with him.

Still laughing, Jeff pushed himself onto one elbow and looked down at her, his hand cupping her cheek. "I can tell that our relationship will never be dull. You're going to keep me on my toes, aren't you?"

Unwilling to define their tentative relationship just then, Autumn rolled away from him and pulled on her robe. "I'll order the pizza."

Jeff reached for his pants. "Tell them to make it snappy, will you? I seem to have worked up quite an appetite."

"BABS, YOU'RE GOING to make yourself sick. Don't you know that pizza isn't good for dogs?"

Autumn smiled at Jeff's serious tone of voice. "Don't tell her that, Jeff. She doesn't know."

He glanced laughingly at her. "What? That pizza's not good for dogs?"

"No. That she *is* a dog."

"Oh. Here, Babs, have another slice of pizza. Want a beer?"

Autumn laughed at his foolishness and munched on her own dinner, her eyes lingering on the lock of dark hair that had again fallen boyishly over Jeff's forehead. She couldn't seem to look away from him. She tried to tell herself a modern woman indulging in a modern, no-strings-attached affair shouldn't be having these giddy, tender feelings, but there didn't seem to be much she could do about it just then. She shrugged those stern thoughts away, telling herself that she was sure she'd be more herself the next day, after the wonder of Jeff's lovemaking had worn off.

Jeff stayed all night, falling asleep only to make love to her again when they woke. If Autumn had thought that the mindless ecstasy she'd felt the first time they'd made love had been a one-time experience, she was proven wrong. It was just as incredible, just as spectacular, the second time. And the third. He left, reluctantly, with long, lingering kisses and murmured promises to see her later.

And then Autumn Sarah Reed, the tough, independent, self-sufficient, liberated woman who never cried, found herself standing in the tub, a steady stream of hot tears mingling with the water from the shower. Because Jeff had made her so very happy. And being that happy terrified her. She could all too easily become addicted to being with Jeff Bradford. And she didn't believe that such happiness could last. There would come a time when she'd have to pay for her pleasure— and the price just might be higher than anything she'd ever given in the past.

"AUTUMN, ARE YOU SURE this isn't too much of an inconvenience?"

"Emily, I'm sure. You said the baby-sitter would be here in half an hour, right? And I'm not due at the wedding until half an hour after that. That gives me plenty of time. Besides, I can get ready with Ryan here. He's no trouble."

"I really hate to ask this, but I promised Mr. Dawson I'd work tonight to finish up those reports."

"Emily, stop it. You've never asked me to baby-sit before, and I've told you several times that I'd be happy to do so. I think I can manage for half an hour. We'll be fine, won't we, Ryan?" Autumn smiled at the child in her arms, receiving a broad grin in return. "Tell Mommy bye-bye."

"Bye-bye," Ryan echoed obediently.

When Emily had gone, Autumn set Ryan on the floor of her bedroom with a cookie and a toddler's spill-proof cup of juice, keeping an eye on him as she applied her makeup for the evening. A friend from work was being married that evening, and she felt obligated to go, even though she'd never been too excited about going to weddings.

"Babs, get away from Ryan's cookie," Autumn warned automatically, her mind still occupied with her plans for the evening. For some reason she was really dreading this particular wedding. Why was she so sure that she would be haunted by thoughts of Jeff during the solemn ceremony?

She hadn't seen Jeff all week. And he wasn't at all happy about it. He'd called every day, only to have her make excuses for why she couldn't see him for another few days. The truth was she was trying to allow enough time to pass for her to get over the lingering aftereffects of their lovemaking on the night she'd returned to Tampa. Finding herself crying in the shower had been such a shock that she'd decided she'd better wait awhile before seeing him again. Make sure that she had firmly reconstructed the emotional barriers between them that he'd so effectively shattered that night. She would *not* fall in love with him, she told herself for the thousandth time. She would *not* allow herself to need him.

She added an extra layer of foundation beneath her eyes to hide the circles that testified to her atypical sleeplessness during the past week. Unfortunately, her body was not as cooperative as her mind in denying her longing for Jeff. Nor was her subconscious. When she'd slept at all, it had only been to dream of him, to replay the most incredible night of her life, to reexperience the feel of him against her, inside her. She cursed under her breath as those thoughts made her hand tremble, smudging her mascara.

She jumped when the telephone rang. She'd told Jeff her plans when he'd called last night to ask her for dinner this evening. He'd responded with growing impatience, demanding to know when he could see her again. Was he calling again already?

Ryan was still working on the cookie as Autumn passed him to answer the extension phone on her bedside table. She patted his sandy head and lifted the receiver. "Hello? Oh, hi, Webb. No, I didn't think you were Jeff," she lied. "My voice was *not* breathless! Stop being such a jerk, Brothers, or you're going to find yourself sitting alone at this wedding. Right, it starts at—Ryan, no!"

Autumn threw the receiver down and made a lunge for the curious child, moments too late to stop him from pulling her curling iron off her dressing table by the cord and picking it up in one chubby fist—by the wrong end. Ryan screamed and dropped the hot appliance, bursting into tears of pain.

Her stomach contracting, Autumn dropped to her knees on the floor beside him. "Let me see, Ryan." She spread his clenched fingers and swallowed. The tiny palms and fingers were an angry red, already beginning to blister. "Oh, you poor baby. God, that must hurt." She pulled the crying child into her arms and rocked him against her shoulder, her own eyes filling with tears of sympathy.

Swiftly unplugging the curling iron, she looked around for her shoes, grateful that she still had on jeans and a T-shirt rather than her robe. Her gaze fell on the telephone receiver lying on the floor, and she snatched it up. Webb was yelling her name, trying to find out what had happened.

"Webb, Ryan's burned his hand," Autumn told him, raising her voice to be heard over the child's noisy sobs. "I'm going to take him to Jeff. Wait for me here, okay?"

Almost sick with guilt and concern, Autumn rushed Ryan out to her car. She didn't have a car seat, of course, but she managed to fasten the seat belt around him, hoping it would be safe enough. He cried most of the way to the clinic, calling for his mother, his hiccuping little sobs wrenching Autumn's heart.

Ryan stopped crying as Autumn took him out of the car. He placed his arms tightly around her neck and buried his face in her shoulder when she paused in front of the clinic reception desk. "Is Jeff here?" Autumn asked the receptionist. "Dr. Bradford, I mean."

"Dr. Bradford is just about to leave for the day. Can someone else help you?"

"Autumn?" Jeff stepped out from the shelves of files behind the reception desk. "I thought I heard your voice. What happened?"

"Oh, Jeff." She'd never been so glad to see anyone in her life. "Ryan burned his hand on my curling iron. It's badly blistered, and I know it's painful."

"Bring him around," Jeff told her, assuming his professional mien, though his tone was still the quiet, deep one that he seemed to reserve for her. "Sheila, call Kelly and ask her to give me a hand."

Autumn had seen Jeff at work before, when she'd worked on the clinic lights, but she was struck anew by his gentleness and patience when he treated Ryan. He talked softly to the child as he spread a thick white cream over the burned skin and then wrapped the entire hand, fingers and all, in soft gauze. Ryan took immediate exception to the latter procedure and didn't hesitate to inform everyone within about a half-mile radius.

"It doesn't hurt much now," Jeff assured Autumn with a half smile, glancing up at her pale face. "He's just mad. Aren't you, pal?" he asked the screaming toddler.

"There," Jeff said a few minutes later. "All done." He picked Ryan up and patted his back, pleased when Ryan stopped crying to curiously investigate the stethoscope dangling from Jeff's pocket, the bandage already forgotten for the moment. Jeff winked at Autumn as he handed the stethoscope over for inspection. "See? He's already forgiven me."

"What did you put on it?" Autumn asked curiously.

"Silvadene Cream. It's practically a miracle drug with burns. Soothes the pain and promotes healing. In a week to ten days the blisters will be gone and Ryan won't even have a scar."

Autumn was preparing to ask another question when she was interrupted by the arrival of Webb and Emily, escorted into the examining room by the young nurse who'd assisted Jeff in treating Ryan. "Is Ryan okay?" Emily asked immediately, rushing to Jeff's side to examine her son. Ryan dove into his mother's arms, contentedly submitting himself for her inspection.

"He's fine," Jeff assured her, explaining again what he had done and telling her how to care for the hand until the burns were fully healed.

"I'm really sorry this happened, Emily." Autumn twisted her hands in front of her, feeling terrible about the entire situation. "One minute he was quietly eating a cookie, and the next he was pulling the curling iron off my dressing table. I didn't even see him move."

"Believe me, Autumn, I understand," Emily replied reassuringly. "Now you know why I've been running myself ragged ever since he learned to walk. He's so darned fast!"

"They all are," Jeff agreed with a chuckle. "Take it from an expert in treating bumps and cuts while listening to distraught mothers saying they just took their eyes off the little darlings for a minute."

"You scared the hell out of me," Webb informed Autumn with a hand pressed dramatically to the area near his heart. "When you screamed and threw the phone down, I nearly had a heart attack."

"Thanks again for coming after me, Webb," Emily told him, giving him a smile that brought a flush to his tanned cheeks. "I know it's not serious, but you were right about me wanting to be here with Ryan. Mr. Dawson said I could finish the reports tomorrow. He's very understanding about my obligations to Ryan."

Autumn didn't ask how Webb had known where to find Emily. She'd suspected that the two had been in close touch for the past few weeks, though neither had been overly talkative on the developing relationship.

"Want to skip the wedding tonight, Autumn?" Webb suggested, glancing down at his casual clothes and her jeans and T-shirt. "We don't really have time to change now, anyway. I'm sure Carl will understand when we explain what happened."

Autumn agreed heartily, welcoming the excuse. Webb and Emily took Ryan home a few minutes later, leaving Autumn alone in the examining room with Jeff. She swallowed a lump in her throat and gave him a shaky smile. "Thanks, Jeff."

"No problem." He stepped closer to her, dropping his hands on her shoulders. "How are *you*? You were so pale earlier that I thought I was going to have to treat you as well as Ryan."

She grimaced. "I just felt so terrible about him hurting himself while I was supposed to be watching him."

Jeff pulled her the few inches remaining between them and wrapped his arms comfortingly around her. "It wasn't your fault, honey. I wasn't exaggerating when I said that accidents like this happen all the time. Actually, you were quite efficient and resourceful. You brought him straight to me without panicking, and you had him calmed down so that we could treat him easily. Until we had to wrap his fingers, of course."

Autumn managed a chuckle. "He hated that, didn't he?"

"They all do. Kids don't like having any part of themselves bound. Too restricting."

She leaned back in his arms and smiled up at him. "You're a very good doctor, Jeff Bradford. If I had kids, I'd want you to be the one taking care of them."

His eyes darkened dramatically. "I fully intend to be the one taking care of your kids, Autumn Reed." He kissed her before she could respond, the embrace starting out light and comforting but quickly turning to searing passion.

Mindful of their surroundings, she gulped and pushed herself hastily out of his arms, refusing to consider the message he'd not so subtly sent her. "I know you were about to leave," she told him, preventing herself from babbling only with a great effort, "so I won't keep you."

"You don't really think I'm going to let you go that easily, do you?" he inquired, watching her with amused understanding. "Now that your other plans have been canceled, you have no excuse for not having dinner with me."

She tried, anyway. "I'm not really dressed to go out." Her hand swept the air between them, indicating the contrast between her jeans and T-shirt and his dress slacks, shirt and tie.

"We'll go to my place," he offered immediately. "I'll put some steaks on the grill."

"I'm not sure that's a good idea," she demurred, knowing what would happen if they were alone at his house.

"Autumn, I'm offering dinner. I won't ravish you."
His eyes glinted suddenly with mischief. "Unless you
want to be ravished, of course," he added.

She stifled a sigh, knowing she was going to accept.
She'd been such an intelligent person before she'd met
Jeff Bradford, she thought. Whatever happened to all
that common sense she'd once prided herself on pos-
sessing?

Jeff drove his BMW home, and Autumn followed in
her Fiero. She talked to him as he started the grill and
put the steaks on, explaining that Emily's baby-sitter
had called earlier to say she'd been detained, which was
why Autumn had been in charge of Ryan when he'd
burned himself. While the steaks were cooking, Jeff ex-
cused himself to change out of his work clothes and into
jeans. Autumn sat by the pool and sipped a cool drink
while he changed. She'd love to swim in that pool, she
thought wistfully, but of course she didn't have a suit
with her. She was musing over tantalizing images of
skinny-dipping there with Jeff when he rejoined her. If
he noticed her heightened color, he wisely made no
comment.

After dinner they watched the episode of Jeff's soap
opera that he'd taped earlier that day. Autumn teased
him about his absorption in the story, though she secretly found his weakness appealing. Of course, she
found everything about him appealing, she admitted
reluctantly. And that was the problem.

"I know you don't like Dr. Noble, but you have to
admit the guy's a pretty good actor," Jeff was saying
when he regained her attention. "I don't know what his
real name is, but he seems ready for feature films to me,
though he's still young."

"His name's Lonnie O'Neal, and he's twenty-nine," Autumn replied without thinking. "And you can bet he's got his eye on Hollywood. He'll jump at the right role when it's offered. He's intended to be a star for years, and he hasn't let anything stand in his way so far. I doubt that he's changed since I knew him."

"Since you knew him?" Jeff repeated, turning on the couch to stare at her. "You never told me you knew him."

She realized what she'd done. Her thoughts had been so caught up in her confused feelings about Jeff that she'd talked without considering her words. "I knew him," she admitted. "Quite well, actually."

Jeff's brows drew sharply downward. "You mean you and he were—"

She shook her head quickly. "Oh, no, not me. Summer. Lonnie and Summer were engaged six years ago. She was crazy about him, though I always thought he was shallow and vain. They were both theater arts majors at UALR—the University of Arkansas at Little Rock—and they planned to become stars together. Then Summer had a motorcycle accident, and Lonnie walked out on her before she even got out of the hospital."

"He did *what*?"

"Dumped her," Autumn answered coldly, surprised that so much anger could remain after such a long time. "Took off for New York while she was still stuck in a wheelchair. Of course, in the long run it was the best thing that ever happened to her. She loves Derek much more than she ever loved Lonnie."

Jeff reached for the remote control and snapped off the television. "I don't think I'll ever watch that show again."

Autumn shrugged. "You don't have to go that far. As you said, Lonnie *is* a very good actor. I'm sure he'll make a big name for himself in the next few years. He's already quite popular with the daytime viewers."

Jeff shook his head emphatically. "I'll never like him now. I can't imagine any man walking out on a woman he claims to love when she needs him the most."

Autumn looked away, knowing full well that Jeff would never walk out on the woman he loved. He would be there by her side, caring for her, encouraging her, supporting her through the hard times. And the woman who loved him would grow to depend on him, need him. Lose herself in him.

"Is that the problem, Autumn?" he asked suddenly, bringing her eyes rapidly back to his face.

"What problem?" she asked, genuinely confused.

"Your fear of commitment. The reason you're so determinedly independent. Was your sister's broken engagement so distressing for you that you decided to avoid the same type of risk yourself?"

"No, Jeff," Autumn answered firmly, though she wondered if she *had* been affected more deeply by Summer's pain than she'd realized. It had been barely a year later that Autumn had broken her own long-standing engagement. "I was engaged once myself. It didn't work out because I'm not the type to make that kind of commitment. I started feeling threatened, smothered by the relationship. I have to be in full control of my own life, not answerable to anyone else. I like it that way."

"You didn't love him." There was no question in Jeff's statement. He looked at her with narrowed eyes, daring her to argue with him.

She shrugged. "I don't know," she confessed. "I thought I did at the time, but I was so young. I tried to change for him, be the kind of clinging, dependent woman that he wanted, but I couldn't do it. He couldn't understand why a woman would want to be an electrician, why I was fascinated by wiring and meters and cables, when he thought I should be reading recipes and attending Tupperware parties. The day after I broke our engagement was the day I felt free, really free, for the first time in my life. I haven't allowed myself to be trapped like that again."

"Love isn't a trap, Autumn," Jeff argued quietly. "And a man who truly loves you wouldn't ask you to change."

"How did we get on this subject, anyway?" She all but jumped to her feet and pushed her hands into her pockets. "You know, after all that's happened today, I'm suddenly exhausted. Thanks for dinner, Jeff, but I think I'll go on home and rest now."

"Don't run from me, Autumn." He rose smoothly and caught her face between his hands, staring intently down at her. "Haven't you understood yet that I don't want to change you or tie you down? I love you, Autumn. I want to share my life with you. I want you to share your life with me. I would never ask you to sacrifice your happiness for me."

"Don't, Jeff. Please." She tensed in pure panic at his words, though she'd been expecting them since the night they'd made love. Which was exactly why she'd been avoiding him ever since.

His hands dropped to her waist, holding her against him. "Autumn, I know you're not ready for vows and commitments. But I won't pretend that all I want from you is a temporary fling. I want forever. I think you've known that from the beginning. I think that's why you've been fighting me every step of the way. You're scared, aren't you, honey?"

"Yes, dammit, I'm scared!" She pulled away from him and walked three quick steps backward, her arms crossed defensively at her waist. "You want too much, Jeff. I can't give you forever."

"Then what *are* you willing to give?" he challenged her.

"An affair. That's all we have, Jeff. An affair. I'm attracted to you, you know that, and I enjoy being with you. But that's all it is."

He shook his head slowly, his eyes almost sad. "You're even running from yourself, aren't you? You won't admit even to yourself that you might possibly need someone."

"I *don't* need anyone!" she answered sharply. "I'm perfectly content to live alone."

"You don't live alone," he pointed out. "You have Babs to keep you from getting too lonely. You even sleep with her." He knew that from experience, having spent a night with Babs curled at his feet in Autumn's bed.

"She's a pet. Lots of people have pets."

"Yes," Jeff agreed. "Loving, caring people who enjoy sharing themselves with others." He lifted his hand in a gesture almost of appeal. "You needed me today, Autumn. And I was there for you. Was it really so bad?"

Her eyes widened, her heart jerking with a kind of shock. She immediately denied his words. "I didn't need you. I needed a doctor, and you're the only one I happen to know personally."

"Autumn, if you'd just needed a doctor, you'd have taken Ryan to the emergency room at Tampa General. It's closer to your place, after all. But you didn't even consider that, did you? You came straight to me. You asked for me at the desk."

"Jeff, you're reading entirely too much into that. I told you, I came to you because you're the only pediatrician I know."

Jeff sighed deeply. "I'm not going to give up, Autumn. You see, I happen to need *you* very badly. And I'm not afraid to admit it. You're the best thing that's ever happened to me. Our night together was the most beautiful night I've ever known. Don't expect me to walk away from that."

"Jeff, what do you want from me?" she cried, her throat tight with suppressed emotion.

"Just give us a chance, Autumn. That's all I'm asking. I won't push you, I won't pressure you, I won't even tell you how much I love you until you're ready to hear it. But don't ask me not to see you again. Please."

She closed her eyes for a moment. "I wish I *could* ask that, Jeff," she admitted at last. "But I can't because I can't stand the thought of not seeing you again. But—" she added quickly, holding up her hand as he took an impetuous step forward "—that doesn't mean I'm ready for more than the affair I've already offered. I'm not."

His eyes were glowing with hope—and the love he didn't try to hide from her. "I don't want an affair. That's not right for me, and we both know it's not right for you, whether you'll admit it or not. So until you're ready to take what I'm offering, we'll see each other as friends, give you a chance to learn that I'm no threat to you. I'm willing to settle for that. For now."

She eyed him skeptically. A platonic friendship? She would have laughed if she hadn't lost her sense of humor sometime during the past half hour. She and Jeff could hardly be in the same room without attacking each other. It had been that way from the moment they'd met. What made him think they could keep their hands off each other now, particularly since they'd already been lovers and knew how good it could be between them? Even now she was quivering with longing for him to touch her. "We can try it, I suppose," she offered doubtfully.

He laughed at the look on her face. "I never said it would be easy, honey. But it'll be worth it when you realize that I'm right about us."

Inhaling deeply, Autumn pushed an unsteady hand through her hair. "For the past five years I've known exactly what I wanted from life, exactly how I intended to accomplish my goals. You confuse me, Jeff. I don't know what I feel or what I want when I'm with you. I can't say that I like being that way. I don't."

"I'll give you time to work out your feelings, Autumn," Jeff promised again. "All the time you need. Because I have faith that when you stop running and give yourself a chance to look without fear at what we have, you'll know we belong together. Not for an affair, but for a lifetime."

9

AUTUMN HAD NEVER been courted before. Her engagement to Steven had come about quite casually, primarily because it seemed to be expected of them. If asked, she would have said she didn't *want* to be courted in the old-fashioned sense of the word. Demeaning, she would have said. Sexist.

For the next few weeks Jeff courted her in true Southern tradition, with flowers and chocolates and patience. He took her to dinner, he called her, he brought her whimsical little gifts wrapped in silver paper. He talked to her, sharing stories of his childhood, his dreams, his hopes. His pain. He came to her after losing one of his favorite little patients in a car accident, and he wasn't ashamed for her to see his tears. She held him in her arms and ached for him, wanting so desperately to take away the pain. She would have made love to him that night—just as she would have any of the nights in the preceding weeks—but again he left her with kisses that short-circuited her brain and a growing frustration that was making sleep impossible and her temper increasingly quick.

And no amount of arguing with herself could convince her that she wasn't loving every minute of his courtship, despite the frustration. She was undoubtedly a fool, she told herself every night before going to bed, but she woke every morning with a sense of anticipation, knowing that she would see or hear from Jeff that day. She stopped accepting dates from anyone else, though she refused to dwell on the implications of that. Outside work she saw only Emily, Ryan and Webb when she wasn't with Jeff.

Jeff's work was, of course, very demanding. More than once during those weeks their dates were interrupted by the demands of his job. She heard him talking patiently on the telephone to hysterical mothers, discussing complicated medical treatments with his partners, discoursing heatedly on parents who abused or neglected their offspring. He was a doctor, first and foremost, a healer, a defender of children. She was a little in awe of that part of him.

He was also a man in love, and he made no effort to hide it. He didn't actually say the words because he'd promised her he wouldn't until she was ready to hear them, but they were in his eyes every time he looked at her, in his touch when he held her or kissed her. She never questioned his sincerity. For some crazy, incomprehensible reason Dr. E. Jefferson Bradford loved Autumn Sarah Reed, electrician, and he fully intended to spend the rest of his life with her.

As time passed, her denials of his intentions grew less forceful. In her weaker moments—and they were coming all too often now—she found herself wondering if Jeff might be right about their future.

And then she'd wake in the night, rigid with dread, unable to breathe, desperately frightened of her growing feelings for him and the heavy sense of inevitability that something would go wrong. She would dream of losing him, and even in her dreams the pain was almost too much to bear. She was beginning to need him, she thought in panic. No, she couldn't allow herself to need him.

And she'd add another emotional brick to the wall she'd built between them.

"You're doing it again." Jeff's words were uttered on a resigned sigh.

Lying in his arms on her couch, she frowned at him in bewilderment, her heart still pounding, breath still ragged from the hungry kisses they'd just shared. "Doing what?" she asked, her voice husky with passion.

"You're pulling away from me."

She looked pointedly down at their intimately entwined bodies, their clothing loosened and disheveled. He was hard and aroused against her; she was trembling with the force of her own desire. "Hardly."

He shook his head, ruffling the lock of hair that had fallen onto his forehead. "Not physically. Emotionally."

She knew now what he meant. He'd been whispering words that were all too close to an outright declaration of his love for her, and she'd found herself coming perilously close to responding in kind. She'd swallowed the words and shut a mental door on her feelings for him, attempting to abandon herself wholly to sensation. How had he known? Was he now adding mind reading to his other talents?

Jeff dropped a quick kiss on her swollen, pouting mouth and pushed himself upright. "It's getting late. Guess I'd better go."

The notorious temper that had been building for the past few weeks, exacerbated by doubts and uncertainties and sheer sexual frustration, finally broke loose. Without even thinking about it, Autumn snatched up a throw pillow that had fallen to the floor earlier and swung it at him. Hard. "You arrogant, obnoxious, un-scrupulous jerk!"

Jeff choked on a startled laugh, caught her hand before she could hit him again and stared down at her as she half sat, half lay on the end of the couch. "Want to tell me what that was about?" he inquired mildly.

"Don't you dare laugh at me!" she shouted, leaping to her feet and angrily straightening her sweater and slacks. "I've had it with you, Bradford, do you hear? What gives you the right to do this to me?"

"What am I doing to you, Autumn?" He leaned back against the cushions, arms stretched out along the back of the couch, his eyes kindling with amusement though he managed not to smile. He knew exactly why she was angry, she thought furiously. *Damn* the man!

"You're driving me crazy, that's what you're doing. And you know it! Spending all your free time with me, kissing me, making me want you and then leaving me on the doorstep with a kiss on the forehead. I won't be blackmailed this way, Jeff."

He wasn't amused now. "I'm not trying to blackmail you, Autumn."

She tossed her head scornfully. "Aren't you? Aren't you using sex to make me say what you want to hear? Don't you think if you tantalize me a little longer I'll say anything to have you make love with me? I hadn't expected such conceit from you, Jeff."

He rose smoothly, stepped up to her and took her shoulders in his hands. He wasn't exactly angry—she'd never seen him angry, she thought fleetingly—but he was definitely annoyed. "That's absurd and you know it. Do you think this past month has been easy for me?"

"I haven't noticed you having any trouble leaving at night," she replied defiantly.

He jerked her against his still-aroused body, his hands falling to her hips to hold her almost painfully against him. "You couldn't be more wrong. Walking away from you has been the hardest thing I've ever had to do. I've taken so many cold showers that I've developed permanent goose bumps and I still wake up at night drenched with sweat and shaking with need for you. God, it's gotten to where it even hurts to kiss you, but when I'm with you, I can't help it. Don't accuse me of trying to make you suffer, Autumn. I'm torturing myself!"

"But *why*?"

He stepped away from her, shoving his hands into the pockets of his navy slacks. "Because I love you," he answered flatly. "And because casual sex with you would hurt much more than none at all."

"It's not casual sex when two people care for each other!" she argued heatedly. "It's called...making love." She said the last words haltingly, her heart stopping at the flame that had suddenly flared in his eyes.

His hands fell again on her shoulders, his grip tight with emotion, though she didn't protest the near pain. "*Do* we care for each other, Autumn?" he asked softly, his words almost a plea.

"Yes," she whispered, unable to lie to him or herself any longer. "Yes, we care for each other. But—"

"Hush," he ordered roughly, pulling her into his arms. "Don't say any more. I told you I was willing to take whatever you were ready to give. As long as you'll admit that what we have is more than physical."

She buried her face in his shoulder, clinging to his shirt. "Don't leave me tonight, Jeff. I...I want you so much." She'd almost said "need." She *wouldn't* say need!

"And I want you, honey. I *need* you," Jeff retorted meaningfully, obviously reading her again. "Just don't accuse me of blackmailing you into making love with me. Please."

She shook her head against him. "No." She knew now that he hadn't been trying to coerce her into saying more than she was ready to say. He'd simply needed reassurance that he was more to her than a good lay. She was continually surprised by this man's vulnerability. And his strength.

She stepped back and took his hand in hers, noting his trembling with a surge of tenderness that took her by surprise. She knew her smile was shaky when she looked up at him, turning to walk with him to her bedroom.

Jeff seemed determined to compensate them both for the weeks of frustration. He made love to her with agonizing slowness, caressing and touching every inch of her—her temples, her throat, her breasts, her stomach, her inner thighs, her ankles. Then he turned her over and explored her back with equal thoroughness, tracing her spine, nibbling at her firm, round cheeks, licking the backs of her knees.

Autumn was shuddering, mindless with need, when he finally gave in to her strangled pleas and ended the torment. He entered her in one smooth thrust, and she rose eagerly to meet him, her knees clasping his hips with all the strength in her healthy young body. His ragged breath and muffled groans were the most beautiful sounds she'd ever heard, and her own soft cries mingled with them in an ancient, wordless duet.

Harder and faster he drove them until neither could hold out any longer against the need for release. Jeff's name was on her lips when Autumn reached that peak, and her own name echoed in her mind after his husky cry. He kept saying it, over and over, as he held her tightly during the descent to sanity. For the first time in twenty-five years she decided she had an absolutely beautiful name. Jeff's voice made it beautiful.

A long time later Autumn stretched, propped herself on one elbow and glared down at his relaxed, contented face. "You sadist."

He chuckled. "Now what have I done?"

"First you make me suffer from abstinence for a month and then you torment me by making love to me so slowly that I lose my mind."

Grinning, he caught her hand and pulled it to his lips. "I suffered from abstinence just as long as you did, you know."

"Your choice."

"No. Not my choice."

She decided not to go into that again. She was feeling too good for a serious discussion just then. Her eyes drifted slowly down his nude length, relishing every gorgeous inch of him. "Then I guess I'll have to make love to you until you lose *your* mind. That'll make us even."

He spread his arms in a gesture of total submission. "Feel free."

Her smile was utterly wicked. "I believe I will."

And she did.

VALENTINE'S DAY CAME a week later. Somehow Autumn had known that Jeff would go all out for that particularly romantic day. She was right. He gave her flowers *and* chocolates *and* an enameled heart pendant on a fine gold chain, and then he took her to dinner at one of the most expensive, exclusive and romantic restaurants in the area. In a whimsically feminist gesture Autumn was waiting with flowers, chocolates and a gold keychain for him when he picked her up for their date.

"I've never had a woman give me flowers and chocolates before," he mused later as he sat across the secluded candle-lit dinner table from her.

Autumn grinned impudently at him. "Did it threaten your masculinity?" she asked.

"Are you kidding? I love flowers. *And* chocolates."

She laughed and shook her head. "I should have known."

"Admit it, Autumn. You're crazy about me," he accused lightly, though his eyes glittered intently in the flickering candlelight.

"I think I'm just crazy," she said with a sigh, implicitly confirming the accusation.

To her relief, Jeff changed the subject. "I can't wait until we dance together after dinner. I love dancing with you when you're wearing that gold thing."

"So that's why you requested that I wear this tonight. You wanted to cop a feel on the dance floor."

Jeff laughed. "You have such a delicate way with words, Autumn."

Her laughter blended with his, and she felt herself slipping even further under his spell. The word "love" hovered in her mind. She could deal with that word, she mused consideringly. Love wasn't nearly as threatening as need. She practiced saying "I love you" in her mind, her eyes dwelling on Jeff's face as he told her a funny story about something Pam had done earlier that day. She wasn't certain when—or if—she'd have the courage to say it aloud, but the words came surprisingly easy to her mind.

She reached across the table and caught his hand, lifting it to her lips in an uncharacteristic display of affection. Jeff ended his story in midsentence, his eyes darkening at the look on her face. "I don't know if we'll make it through an entire dance," he told her hoarsely.

Rubbing her cheek against his knuckles, she smiled at him. "I don't mind if you don't."

And they didn't.

AUTUMN'S DOORBELL CHIMED at just after six on the following Wednesday evening. Stifling a moan, she started to rise to answer the door, but Webb stopped her with a firm hand pressed to her shoulder. "Don't you move," he ordered her sternly. "I'll get it."

"Webb, you're driving me insane. Why don't you go away?" she asked petulantly.

"This is the thanks I get for taking care of you when you're wounded?" Webb demanded indignantly, throwing her an exaggeratedly insulted look over his shoulder as he turned the doorknob. "Oh, it's you, Jeff."

From the angle at which she was lying on her couch, Autumn could see Jeff quite clearly. She watched his eyes narrow at the man who opened Autumn's door. "Are you here again, Webb? I think you and I are going to have to talk."

Autumn blinked at the very male tone and lifted her head from the pillow Webb had insisted on fetching for her a few minutes earlier. It had been a hellish day. All she needed now was for Jeff, of all people, to turn macho on her. Though she'd talked to him several times on the telephone, this was the first time she'd seen him since their Valentine's Day date, a night that had been pure magic from dinner to the hours of lovemaking that had followed. Usually he called before coming over.

Wouldn't you know he'd drop by unexpectedly on this of all evenings? she thought ruefully.

"Why don't we save it for another time?" Webb said smoothly, his tone acknowledging the challenge in the other man's voice. "Autumn's been hurt, and I—"

"*What?*" Jeff pushed abruptly past Webb to swiftly cross the room and drop to his knees beside the couch. "Autumn, are you all right? What happened?"

"Jeff, it's nothing. Really. Just a stupid little accident." She stopped with a sigh as she realized that she was wasting her breath. Jeff had gone into doctor mode, already examining the ugly bruise on her forehead and the ragged, three-inch-long cut on her left forearm that had been neatly closed by a half-dozen or so stitches. "Jeff, I've seen a doctor," she protested when he automatically checked her pupils. "Webb took me to the emergency room at Tampa General. I don't have a concussion."

"What happened?" he repeated, and she was amazed to realize that he'd gone pale beneath his tan.

She attempted a light, soothing tone. "I bumped my head and cut my arm at work this afternoon. It wasn't serious, so don't—"

"She almost killed herself," Webb broke in curtly, dropping into a chair and watching the couple in front of him with interest. "If her reflexes weren't so fast, she would have been at least badly injured."

Thoroughly irritated, particularly when she noted that Jeff's eyes had widened considerably, Autumn glared at Webb. "Shut up, Webb, and let me tell him."

Ignoring Autumn, Jeff turned to Webb. "No, you tell me. What happened?" he asked for the third time, growing visibly less patient by the moment.

Paying no attention to Autumn's attempt to interrupt, Webb explained succinctly. "She was running conduit in the mall we're working on, standing on scaffolding twenty feet off the floor. She needed to reach out a little farther than her safety belt would allow her to go, so she unsnapped it." He gave Autumn a stern glance and continued. "She turned too quickly, bumped her head on a metal beam and lost her balance, cutting her arm on an air-conditioning duct when she reached out to grab something to hold on to. She managed to catch herself just as one of the guys got to her to help her down, but she came so damn close to falling that my heart stopped."

"My God." Jeff inhaled sharply and rested his forehead against Autumn's for a moment before raising his head to look at her intently. "You're sure you're okay?"

"I'm sure," she answered steadily, deciding not to mention that she was in a great deal of pain from her arm and her pounding head. The shot she'd been given earlier was wearing off, and her arm felt as if it was on fire.

She should have known she couldn't fool a doctor—this doctor, in particular. His blue eyes narrowed, and she suspected that he was taking complete inventory of the circles under her eyes, her pallor and the slight sheen of moisture on her forehead. "What did they give you for pain?" he demanded.

Again Webb answered. "The pain medication is on the coffee table. She refused to take it when I tried to give it to her a few minutes ago."

"Webb, would you go home?" Autumn exploded wrathfully, her small tantrum sending painful fireworks off in her head. "Thank you for everything, but please go away."

With a deep, soulful sigh Webb unfolded himself from his chair and rose, crossing the room to drop a light kiss on Autumn's forehead. "Okay, I'm going. You've got a genuine doctor here to take care of you now, so I can leave with a clear conscience. Don't let me see you at work until at least Monday, you hear?"

"I hear," Autumn muttered, her head moving restlessly on the pillow. Jeff had disappeared into her kitchen, quite probably after a glass of water. It seemed she'd be taking the pain pills after all. Why wouldn't everyone go away and let her die in peace? she bemoaned silently as Webb let himself out the front door.

"Not a very gracious patient, are you, honey?" Jeff's voice was amused as he sat carefully on the edge of the couch at her side.

"No, I'm not a gracious patient," Autumn grumbled, glaring at him. "I'm ill-tempered and foul-mouthed and horrible. I refuse to do what anyone tells me, and I don't want those pills because they'll make me loopy and I hate being that way. And I don't like being called honey!"

To her surprise, Jeff laughed softly and leaned over to place a soft kiss on her sullen mouth. "Trying to scare me away, Autumn?"

"Yes," she answered recklessly. "If you had any sense at all, you'd admit that I'm totally wrong for you, take to your heels and never see me again."

"And if *you* had any sense at all, you'd realize that you are exactly right for me. I'm not going anywhere. But I will stop calling you honey. I didn't know you disliked it. You should have told me long before this."

She bit her lip, closing her eyes and trying to fight down a surge of disappointment at the thought of never hearing him call her honey again. Lord, what was the matter with her?

"Take the pills, Autumn."

"Not now, Jeff. I'll take them later."

"Now, Autumn."

Her eyes flew open at his tone. When and how had sweet, smiling young Dr. Bradford learned to inject pure steel into his voice? His gaze met hers, and her mouth opened automatically to take the small pills he was holding to her lips.

"That was sneaky and underhanded," she complained when she'd swallowed the pills with a sip of the water he'd brought her.

"What was?" The steel was gone now, replaced by the familiar gentle amusement.

"I didn't know that you could sound like that."

"It comes in handy with stubborn patients." He set the glass on the coffee table and brushed a stray curl away from her forehead. "You'll feel better in a few minutes. You have to expect pain from a cut like this, but there's no need to suffer unnecessarily."

"So you think I'm acting like one of your patients, do you? Are you calling me a child?"

Jeff chuckled. "You're determined to pick a fight, aren't you, hon—uh, Autumn? It won't work, you know."

She sighed and closed her eyes. "I am perfectly capable of taking care of myself. I thought you and Webb understood that. So how come you've both been treating me like a helpless airhead?"

"Autumn, we care about you and you're hurt. It has nothing to do with your capability or intelligence. Now why don't you come down off that feminist soapbox and admit that you'd do the same for Webb—or me, I hope—if the tables were turned. You would, wouldn't you?"

Autumn immediately had a mental picture of Jeff hurt and in pain, and she admitted to herself that she would, indeed, do whatever she could to help him. Webb, too, she added in a quick afterthought. And, dammit, she *was* acting like a whining child. She sighed again and looked apologetically up at him. "Yes, I would. I'm sorry I've been so grouchy."

"S'okay. I'm a lousy patient myself. All doctors are, you know."

Slowly relaxing, she settled more comfortably against the pillow. "I wasn't expecting to see you tonight."

"I know. I was going to call first, but I couldn't wait that long. I wanted to see you."

"As you can see, I'm not very good company tonight."

"That's okay. Just lie back and let me take care of you. Are you hungry? Would you like for me to make you a bowl of soup?"

"Thanks, but that's not necessary. I'm not very hungry."

"Actually, I am. I'll make us a light supper, and maybe you can eat just a little."

"Jeff, really, you don't have to stay."

"I know I don't have to stay," he answered gently. "But I want to. Do you honestly want me to leave?"

She should say yes. She didn't like being taken care of, as he well knew. If she asked, he would leave and she would be alone. Wishing he were still there. "No," she whispered reluctantly. "I don't want you to leave. Not . . . if you really want to stay for a while."

He kissed her, not quite as gently as before, though she sensed that he was exerting quite a bit of restraint to hold back even that much. "Thank you," he told her, his voice rough. "I'll go make that soup now."

She closed her eyes wearily, listening to him moving around in the other room, his deep voice speaking softly to Babs. And she was suddenly fiercely glad that he was there, that her cross mood hadn't driven him away. Still very much aware of his presence, she allowed herself to drift into sleep.

JEFF SWALLOWED the last bite of the sandwich he'd made to go with his soup and reached for his canned cola, his eyes never leaving Autumn's face. She was sleeping restlessly, obviously in pain despite the pills he'd insisted she take. She'd be more comfortable in bed, he decided, setting the can on a coaster and rising to carry his soup bowl into the kitchen. She was liable to bite his head off if she woke up and found him tucking her in, but the thought didn't particularly disturb him. He grinned, thinking of her obvious surprise that her irritability hadn't sent him running earlier. How many men had she frightened away with her fiery temper? And didn't she know by now that he wasn't intimidated by it?

So cautious, he thought, kneeling at her side again and pressing the lightest of kisses to her moist forehead. So wary. So terribly afraid of getting involved or admitting that she might occasionally need someone. Someday, he vowed as he slipped his arms beneath her to lift her, she was going to freely admit that she needed someone. Him.

She didn't rouse when he carried her into the bedroom. He couldn't help comparing this time to the first

night he'd made love to her, when she'd snuggled into
his shoulder—after making sure that he knew she was
doing so by her choice—and given herself up to passion. He felt his body hardening in reaction to the
breathtaking memories and regretfully shook his head.
There would be no such pleasure on this night. But he
intended to sleep beside her, anyway. There was no way
he was leaving her alone tonight.

He rummaged in her dresser drawers, looking for
something more comfortable for sleeping than the shirt
and jeans she was wearing. His brow lifted with interest when he came across a slinky black satin-and-lace
nightgown among the more practical T-shirts. Not
Autumn's usual style, he thought, an unexpected surge
of jealousy rippling through him for the second time
that evening. He hadn't liked having Autumn's door
opened by Webb, but he absolutely hated the idea of
Autumn's wearing this filmy garment for anyone but
him. Then his eye caught the tag hanging from the back
of the nightgown and he relaxed. She'd never worn it.

Smiling broadly, he folded the gown back into the
drawer and pulled out an oversized white T-shirt. She
would wear the black gown for him soon, but he
wanted her fully conscious when he took it off her, he
thought cockily.

He undressed her with great care, conscious of the
tenderness that almost overwhelmed him at taking care
of her. He was comfortable, as many men were not,
with the gentle, nurturing side of himself, the side that
had led him into pediatric medicine and showed itself
every day in his work. But there was a difference in
these feelings for Autumn. This was a tenderness mixed
with respect, admiration, amusement, passion. Love.
He'd never been in love before. He'd been waiting for

Autumn, he thought whimsically, unable to resist looking at her for a moment before covering her lovely body with the soft T-shirt.

He tucked her under the covers, arranging her injured arm across her stomach. He winced at the angry red swelling around the stitches, his insides knotting as he pictured the accident. She could so easily have been killed or seriously injured. He didn't like the idea of her working in such a risky field. Construction workers were so often killed in falls or other work-related accidents. He wished...

No. Jeff sat quietly on the side of the bed, looking down at the woman he loved. She enjoyed her job, the challenges of working with her hands, just as he enjoyed his vocation. If she'd originally chosen to be an electrician as a form of rebellion against traditional roles, she'd stayed with it because she liked it. And he wouldn't make the mistake of trying to change her. There would be no faster way to lose her.

Besides, as he'd assured her repeatedly, he didn't want to change her. He loved her. If only he could make her believe him.

She didn't even stir when he kissed her. "I love you," he murmured, willing the words into her dreams. And then he stood, clearing his throat of emotion. "Well, Babs," he addressed the tiny poodle looking expectantly up at him from the floor. "Want to watch some TV?"

10

AUTUMN STIRRED, frowned and slowly opened her eyes. She had no idea what time it was. For that matter, she had no idea how she'd ended up in her bed when she distinctly remembered falling asleep on the couch.

She moved her injured arm and winced. *Jeff.* Lifting her head, she could hear the muted sound of the television coming from the other room. He hadn't left.

She dropped her head back down and moaned. God, she felt like an idiot. Sure, accidents like that happened every day, but not usually to her—not since she'd been a daredevil tomboy tumbling from one scrape into another. She was always so careful, determined that no one could accuse her of being unqualified for her job.

Her mouth tasted awful. She was hungry. And she needed to use the bathroom. She forced herself upright, flinching at the protest from jarred, sore muscles. She blinked when she realized that she was wearing only a white sleep shirt over her bikini panties. Jeff had undressed her, she realized, oddly embarrassed that he'd seen her so vulnerable without her knowledge. Her next thought was a self-reproachful question. How could she have slept through *that*?

A few minutes later she stood in the doorway to the bedroom and looked at the man sprawled comfortably on her couch watching TV with her dog curled on his knee. She'd run a brush through her hair in the bathroom, but she hadn't wanted to attempt putting on her robe over the sore, swollen arm. She couldn't help being a bit self-conscious standing in front of him in the thin, midthigh-length cotton shirt, even though she knew he'd recently seen her in much less. As she had him.

"How're you feeling?" he asked, watching her closely as she crossed the room to sit beside him.

"Better, I guess," she admitted. "My head doesn't hurt as badly now. I just feel so stupid."

He ran his knuckles lightly down her cheek. "Don't, Autumn. Everyone makes mistakes sometimes." He held out the hand he'd touched her with, displaying a thin white scar across the palm—a scar she'd noticed with curiosity but had never gotten around to asking him about. "I did that cleaning a fish after a fishing trip with Julian last summer. Julian yelled at me the whole time he was sewing me up. My patients all made fun of me for having to take care of them with a bandage on my hand because I'd cut myself with a knife. Pam told me I couldn't be trusted with anything sharp and threatened to take my medical bag away from me."

Autumn chuckled despite herself. "Gave you a hard time, did they?"

"Did they ever. Will the guys at work tease you when you go back?"

She grimaced. "My friends will. Those few who don't believe a woman should be an electrician will use this as evidence of their sexist arguments."

"You didn't hurt yourself because you're a woman," Jeff stated flatly. "You hurt yourself because you were momentarily careless. I doubt there's one of them who hasn't done something similar at one time or another."

Autumn tilted her head and smiled at him. "Somehow I wasn't expecting this from you."

"Oh?" He looked surprised. "What were you expecting?"

"A lecture about how dangerous my work is," she answered promptly. "Maybe a tactful suggestion that I go into another line."

Wearing his most innocent expression and fully determined that she'd never know he'd briefly wished that very thing, Jeff shook his head reproachfully. "You should have known better."

"Mmm. Well, anyway, you've almost made up for coming across like a dictator about the pain pills."

He glanced at his watch. "Speaking of which, it's time for another dose. You slept for four hours."

"Jeff . . ." she wailed.

"Don't make me spoil your decent mood by having to play the dictator again," Jeff warned her with a smile. "That last dose will be wearing off any time now, and you'll be in pain again. There's no need for that."

"I hate taking drugs," she muttered, shifting the arm that was already beginning to throb, to her annoyance.

"This is just a mild painkiller," he answered soothingly. "You'll have to take them tomorrow, but after that you won't need them. Believe me, honey, I wouldn't insist that you take them if I thought they were bad for you. Are you hungry? Want me to warm up some soup?"

"I *am* hungry," she admitted, aware of the endearment and the warm glow that accompanied it. She spoke quickly. "And I'm thirsty. But I can get it."

"Take one step toward that kitchen and I'll really show you macho," Jeff told her humorously. "I'll bring you a tray. You can talk to Babs while I'm getting it. She's been worried about you." He deposited the drowsy dog on the couch beside Autumn and stood. He paused in the doorway to the kitchen, looking back apologetically. "Oh, I called you honey again, didn't I? Sorry, it just slipped out."

Autumn flushed and looked quickly down at Babs. "That's okay. I don't really dislike it all that much. I was just in a bad mood earlier."

She sensed his smile, though she could not make herself meet his eyes. "I'll get your dinner," Jeff said softly, wisely not commenting on her statement.

THE FIRST THING AUTUMN SAW when she woke the next morning was Jeff's smile. Her mind still foggy with the remnants of sleep, she decided that there was nothing she'd rather see first thing in the morning, though she had no intention of telling him that. "Have you been staring at me for very long?" she asked huskily, not sounding nearly as stern as she'd intended.

Head propped on one elbow, he looked down at her, his smile widening. "Awhile. You're beautiful when you're asleep. Did you know that? You're beautiful when you're awake, too."

She rolled her eyes and smothered a yawn. "I don't feel beautiful. I feel like—"

"Watch your mouth," he said quickly, teasingly. "Beautiful women shouldn't use such language."

"Now *that's* a sexist remark." Autumn tried to frown at him, an admittedly difficult task since he looked young and heart-stoppingly sexy with his dark hair tousled over his forehead, his eyes heavy-lidded, bare chest glistening in the sunlight streaming through the bedroom window. The shadow of his morning beard did not detract from the attractive picture—just the opposite, in fact. Her heart started a crazy tap dance, accompanied by the steadily increasing rhythm of her pulse.

"Sorry. How's your arm?" Jeff inquired solicitously.

She moved it experimentally. "Ouch."

"Sore, huh?"

"Yeah." She noticed that the sheet had slipped down around his hips, revealing the tops of low-slung blue briefs. She immediately forgot all about her arm.

"You should take one of your pain pills."

Autumn wondered if she'd imagined that his voice had gotten a bit hoarse. She studied him through her lashes. He seemed to be suddenly fascinated with the front of her T-shirt. The thin white T-shirt was stretched tightly across her chest by the position in which she was lying. She inhaled, pleased to note that his eyes immediately glazed.

She hadn't protested when he'd informed her the night before that he was going to spend the night, even though she'd known he was staying to take care of her if she needed him. Although she'd firmly believed she was capable of taking care of herself, she'd allowed him to stay quite simply because she hadn't wanted him to go. Last night she hadn't felt like doing anything more than sleeping in his arms. This morning she was feeling much better. She smiled slowly at him.

Jeff cleared his throat forcefully. "Stop looking at me like that, Autumn Reed."

She reached out with her good arm and circled a tempting, flat brown nipple with the very tip of one finger. "Like what, Jeff?" she asked with not-very-deceptive innocence.

"Autumn, you're injured, remember?"

Her finger trailed lower, following a thin line of hair to the point where it disappeared beneath the sheet. "I'm not dead, Jeff."

He caught her hand just as it was about to burrow beneath the sheet. "You're not making it easy for me to be noble," he told her, and his voice was definitely hoarse.

"What makes you think I want you to be noble?" She stroked his hair-roughened leg with one bare foot.

Jeff groaned and closed his eyes. "I sure hope you know what you're doing, honey."

"I know exactly what I'm doing, *honey*," she murmured wickedly, and leaned forward to kiss him, her hand escaping his to continue its exploration under the sheet.

"That you do, Autumn," Jeff muttered with a sharp inhalation, willingly abandoning himself to her hungry caresses. And when she'd pushed him past the point of control, he returned the favor, always careful of her injury but driving her without mercy to the boundaries of sanity. At some point they crossed that line together, and the shared madness was glorious.

"I wasn't going to do that," Jeff accused her when he'd recovered. "You made me lose my chance to show you how strong and considerate and self-sacrificing I can be."

Autumn chuckled weakly, still a bit dazed. "You keep forgetting that I like you best when you're *not* perfect."

Something flickered across his face at the word "like," but it was carefully disguised. "Want some breakfast?" he asked.

"Don't you have to work today?"

He shook his head. "It's Thursday, remember? My day off. I've got my beeper with me, if they need me."

"You don't have to spend your day off waiting on me, Jeff. Really, I'm fine. As you should know by now."

"Yes, I know you're fine. But I'm still staying. I'm going to spoil you so thoroughly that you'll never want me to leave," he informed her smugly, climbing out of the bed and padding toward the bathroom.

Autumn watched him with a slight frown. That, she thought nervously, was exactly what she was afraid of. That she would never want him to leave.

Much later she was to realize how strange it was that she could so thoroughly enjoy a day at home with a sore, bruised forehead and a throbbing, stitched-up arm. She'd always hated being at all incapacitated, rarely took a sick day from work unless she was simply too ill to crawl out of bed. But then she'd never had Jeff to entertain her on a sick day before. If she wasn't careful, she thought sometime during the afternoon, she was in danger of becoming a hypochondriac. As Jeff had promised, he'd thoroughly spoiled her.

He pampered her, he teased her, he kissed her repeatedly. He lost two games of chess to her, then soundly defeated her at Scrabble.

"A-n-t-i-c. Antic. Write down my points, Jeff."

"Great! I can finally use this X. X-e-r-a-n-t-i-c. Xerantic. That gives me—"

"Xerantic! There's no such word!"

"Of course there is," Jeff answered, looking insulted. "It means causing dryness."

She frowned skeptically at him, but he seemed completely serious. "Okay. I guess I'll believe you."

A moment later she protested again. "Now, come on, Jeff. Surely you're not going to try to convince me that 'xanthosis' is a real word."

Again the wounded look. "But it is."

"Oh, yeah? What does it mean?"

"Well, actually, it's a yellowish discoloration seen in some malignant tumors and degenerating tissues. 'Xanthous,' of course, meaning yellow and —"

"Never mind," Autumn sighed, staring glumly down at her own letters—she'd planned to spell "table" next. "I should have known better than to play Scrabble with a doctor."

Jeff gave her one of the wicked, piratical grins that always took her by surprise coming from him. "We could put this up and just play 'doctor.'"

Autumn glanced up through her lashes and dumped her tiles into the box. "I do like the way your mind works, Dr. Bradford."

"JEFF?" AUTUMN POKED at the man resting at her side as a sudden thought occurred to her.

"Mmm?" he mumbled without opening his eyes.

Clutching the sheet to her bare breasts, she struggled upright, wincing when her movements jarred her arm. "Wake up. I want to ask you something."

He sighed and rolled onto his back, one arm behind his head, his eyes finally open. "What?"

"What's the *E* for?"

He frowned, puzzled. "What's *what*?"

"The *E*. In your signature. E. Jefferson Bradford. It just occurred to me that I'm sleeping with a man whose first name I don't even know."

Jeff groaned. "This is the important question you just had to ask?"

"Yep." She smiled enticingly down at him. "What's your first name, Jeff?"

He rolled onto his side, turning his back to her. "I'm going to take a nap. Wake me in an hour, at six, and I'll make dinner for us."

"Jeff!" She grabbed his shoulder and pulled him onto his back again. "You haven't answered my question."

"I know. And I'm not going to."

"You won't tell me your first name?" she demanded indignantly. "Why not? You know all my names."

He gave her a bland smile and reached up to pat her cheek. "I'll tell you my first name on the day we get married."

"You'll ... *what*?" Openmouthed, she stared down at him.

"You see, it's like this," he continued calmly. "I hate my first name. I never tell anyone my first name. Only members of my immediate family know what it is. I'll tell you when you're part of my immediate family."

And then he rolled over.

Autumn glared at the tanned width of his back, imagining all the painful things she could do to it. *This* was his idea of a marriage proposal? *This* from the man who'd courted her with flowers and candy and Valentines? Whatever happened to getting down on one knee and begging?

Not that she wanted him to propose, she assured herself hastily. She hadn't even gotten around yet to admitting that she loved him. She certainly wasn't ready to consider marriage. But he could have asked!

"I," she informed him coldly, "am going to take a shower. Enjoy your nap."

"Take a bath," he muttered in response. "And keep that arm dry."

She let out her breath in an irritated huff and slipped from the bed, deciding to take a very long bath.

The water had just stopped running in the bathroom when the telephone rang. "Jeff, would you get that?" Autumn called. "Tell whoever it is I'll call back later."

Jeff reached out for the receiver on the bedside table, propping himself against the pillows. He expected the caller to be Webb, checking on Autumn. "H'lo," he greeted, stifling a sleepy yawn.

There was a pause, and then a woman's voice asked hesitantly, "Is this Autumn Reed's number?"

"Yes, it is," Jeff replied, straightening and pushing a hand through his hair. "She can't come to the phone right now. Can I give her a message?"

"This is her sister, Spring. Your name wouldn't be Jeff, would it?"

Jeff lifted an eyebrow. "Yes, I'm Jeff Bradford. Has Autumn mentioned me?" he asked, pleased with the idea. He could never be sure with Autumn.

"Of course. You're the pediatrician she's been dating."

"That's right. And you're the pregnant optometrist," he said with a grin.

Spring laughed. "Well, yes, I guess I am. It's nice to meet you, Jeff. In a manner of speaking, of course."

"It's nice to meet you, too. Maybe we can do this in person someday soon."

"I'd like that. So how is my sister?"

Taking the question literally, Jeff told Spring about the accident, reassuring her that Autumn would be fine in a few days.

"This sounds so familiar." Spring sighed. "You wouldn't believe the number of times my parents had to rush her to the closest emergency room when she was a kid. She was always breaking something or cutting something or spraining something. Lucky for her that she doesn't scar badly or she'd look like a patchwork quilt."

Intrigued, Jeff cradled the receiver more comfortably against his ear. "Accident-prone, was she?"

"More accurately a daredevil. There wasn't anything she was afraid to try, especially if someone actually dared her. She'd climb trees, jump off roofs, ride unbroken horses, whatever took her fancy at the time. Daddy threatened to tie her up and keep her in a closet, only letting her out on a leash."

Jeff could picture Autumn as a redheaded tomboy, climbing trees and jumping off roofs. He was glad that Spring couldn't see his undoubtedly besotted grin as he turned his eyes toward the closed bathroom door. "Why does this not surprise me?"

"Did she tell you about the time she broke her hand?"

"I know she broke some bones, but she didn't tell me how she did it."

"Oh, well..." And Spring related the story with great relish, making Jeff laugh heartily.

"You're kidding!"

"No. Sure you still want to go out with her?"

Jeff sobered abruptly. "I want to marry her," he informed Autumn's sister, knowing that Autumn would strangle him if she knew he'd announced his intentions to her family. But he figured he needed all the allies he could get.

"Does she know?" was all Spring asked.

"She's getting the message."

"Good luck, Jeff. You've got your work cut out for you. She's scared to death of getting tied down like that."

"I don't intend to tie her down. I intend to set her free," Jeff stated unequivocally. He didn't explain that he meant to set Autumn free from her fears and insecurities, but Spring seemed to understand, anyway.

"Now I really can't wait to meet you. I plan to give you a big hug as soon as I see you," Spring told him with obvious approval.

"I'll look forward to it. I'll tell Autumn you called, Spring."

"Okay, thanks. Bye, Jeff."

Score one for his side, Jeff thought with a smile as he replaced the receiver. He'd known he'd like Autumn's family when she'd first told him about them. He was genuinely eager to meet them. Just as he'd become impatient to introduce Autumn to his own family.

Climbing out of the bed, he pulled on his briefs and jeans, leaving the button at the waist undone, and strolled into the bathroom.

Autumn was soaking as comfortably as possible in the hot water, her injured arm propped on the side of the tub. She lifted an eyebrow at him. "You said you were going to take a nap."

"I thought you might need help washing your back." He perched on the edge of the tub and smiled down at her, his eyes taking in every inch of the luscious body exposed to him through the clear water. "You look good wet."

She didn't quite blush, but Jeff sensed with amusement that she'd made an effort not to do so. No sophisticated flirt, his love, and he wouldn't have her any other way. "Can it," she muttered with her usual sweet charm.

Jeff laughed and lifted her right hand to his lips, licking a drop of water from her knuckles before kissing them, delighted when the gesture made her shiver. He caressed the hand, his thumbs tracing the faint ridges of once-broken bones he'd discovered on the day they'd met—almost four months earlier, he realized. "You never told me how you broke your hand."

Sternly lifting eyelids that had gone heavy, she straightened in the tub and pulled her hand from his. "I told you, it was an accident."

"You know what I'd bet? I'd bet you broke it punching somebody. Maybe you found a football jock twice your size picking on a scrawny kid and you walloped him one."

Autumn sighed deeply and reached for a towel. "You've been talking to one of my sisters. Which one called?"

Laughing, Jeff stood and helped her out of the tub. "Spring. Did you really try to break some kid's jaw?"

"Yes, I did," she answered reluctantly. "And I ended up breaking two bones in my hand. But it was worth it. He was an obnoxious bully."

"Guess you learned your lesson about taking on someone bigger than you."

"Nope. But I did learn how to throw a punch without breaking my hand," she answered sweetly. "Perhaps you should take that as a warning."

"You wouldn't hit me," he replied casually, wrapping her snugly in the oversized towel. "You love me."

"That doesn't mean I won't be inclined to deck you occasionally," she retorted unhesitatingly. "In fact, I—" She stopped, staring at him. He knew she had seen the hope that had flared to life in him at her words. "Dammit, Jeff!"

He lifted a hand to her damp, flushed cheek, almost afraid to breathe. "Do you love me, Autumn?"

"You pick the oddest times to get into these discussions. You could at least let me dry off and put some clothes on," she stalled.

"Do...you...love...me...Autumn?" he asked again, spacing the words deliberately.

"Yes!" she all but spat at him, her eyes narrowed furiously. "I love you, all right? Now if you'll excuse me, I'm going to get dressed." And she whirled and almost bolted from the bathroom, avoiding any actions or discussions related to her unwilling confession.

Jeff laughed quietly and ran an unsteady hand through his disheveled hair. He should have known, he thought bemusedly. He should have known Autumn would throw the words at him like a hand grenade, angry with him for forcing them out of her. But she'd said them and she meant them. She loved him.

His amusement faded abruptly. It still wasn't enough. There was still something she was holding back. He wished to heaven he knew what it was. And why couldn't he just settle for what she was willing to give?

He knew why. He wanted it all. As Spring had said, he had his work cut out for him.

Though Autumn clearly expected further discussion about the subject of her love for him, and just as clearly dreaded it, Jeff carefully made no reference to the scene in the bathroom. Instead, he cooked dinner and kept the conversation light and amusing as they ate, encouraging her to tell him more about her childhood with her sisters in rural Arkansas. After dinner they watched a television movie, and then he told her he had to go. "Sure you'll be okay tonight?"

"I'll be fine," she assured him. He wondered if he was imagining her reluctance to see him leave only because he wanted to see it. "Thanks for everything, Jeff."

"My pleasure. I'll always be here when you need me," he told her softly, dropping a kiss on her forehead.

He didn't miss her sudden stiffening. "Well, I could have managed just fine alone," she told him carefully. "But I enjoyed your company. And your cooking," she added with a weak smile.

"You're not planning to work tomorrow, are you?" Even to him his voice sounded suddenly strained, but she only looked quickly at him and shook her head.

"No, Webb told me to take off until Monday. Even then he probably won't let me do anything except serve as general gofer until my stitches are out."

"Good. I'll call you tomorrow, then."

"All right. Good night, Jeff."

"Good night, Autumn." He pulled her into his arms and kissed her lingeringly. "I love you," he whispered when he released her, and then he left hurriedly, while he could still make himself go.

So now he knew, he thought a long time later, staring into his pool as he sat beside it, unable to sleep. Now he knew what was missing. Autumn loved him, but she still refused to admit that she needed him. And until she did, they could never have the relationship he wanted them to have. There would always be a part of herself that she held back from him. She didn't trust him enough to allow herself to need him.

It hurt. It hurt a lot. Because he needed her so desperately, and he was terribly afraid that he would never really have her.

OUTWARDLY THEIR RELATIONSHIP changed little during the next two weeks. They spent their free time together, sometimes alone, sometimes with Jeff's friends or Autumn's. They attended the Jeremy Kane performance and were both caught up in the magic the skilled entertainer wove with his audience. Afterward they went to Jeff's house and made love, and their magic was even more powerful than Kane's.

But Jeff was still painfully conscious of the restraints between them. He couldn't stop himself from telling Autumn how much he loved her. He murmured the words when he kissed her good-night, spoke them into the telephone when he couldn't see her, gasped them in the throes of passion. At first she'd been hesitant to respond in kind, but as the days passed, it seemed to become easier for her. She could tell him she loved him. She would not tell him that she needed him.

It was the middle of March before Jeff finally convinced Autumn to go with him to Sarasota for a weekend with his family. It was his parent's thirty-fifth wedding anniversary, and their friends were giving them a small reception on Saturday evening. "How will you introduce me?" Autumn asked him warily.

"I'll tell everyone that you're the electrician I've been sleeping with," he returned without a beat.

"Jeff!"

He laughed. "Well, really, Autumn, how do you *think* I'm going to introduce you? I thought I'd tell everyone that your name is Autumn Reed. Does that meet with your approval?"

"I just don't want you to give your parents the wrong idea about us," she answered carefully. "It's . . . it's not like we're engaged or anything."

"Honey, just because I'm taking you to meet my parents doesn't mean they'll think we're engaged," he argued, though she fancied there was a bit of wistfulness behind his words.

"Then you've taken other women home to meet them?" She spoke lightly, trying to hide that she hated the very idea.

"Well, no, but—"

"So they *will* think I'm someone special to you."

"Autumn." He took her hands in his, staring patiently down at her. "My parents know all about you. They know that I'm crazy in love with you and have been since I met you in October. They know that I hope to spend the rest of my life with you. They also know that there is no formal engagement between us, so you needn't worry about that."

"You mean you told them—"

"I'm very close to my parents," Jeff interrupted firmly. "I don't keep important events in my life secret from them. I'd hardly keep quiet about you."

"Oh, Jeff, what am I going to do with you?" She sighed in resignation.

"I could answer that in detail," he answered slowly, his warm smile lighting his eyes, "or I could take it as rhetorical and go on to the next subject."

"You'd better take it as rhetorical."

"Consider it done. Will you go to Sarasota with me next weekend?"

"Yes, I'll go." She swallowed and tried to hide her attack of nerves behind bluff bravado. "But if you introduce me even once as 'the little woman'. . ." She let her voice trail off meaningfully.

He grinned. "How about 'my better half'?"

"You'd die."

"I'll keep that in mind." He pulled her into his arms. "I'll just call you the beautiful, fascinating, stubborn, capable, intriguing and oh-so-elusive woman that I love. How does that sound?"

She wrapped her arms around his neck. "Better just call me Autumn."

"Autumn," he murmured and kissed her. "Autumn." He kissed her again, longer this time. "Autumn . . . Autumn . . . Autumn."

"Jeff," she whispered after the last lingering kiss, and pulled his head back down to hers.

11

KATHLEEN BRADFORD WAS an attractive, fifty-eight-year-old woman who was still deeply in love with her handsome, sixty-year-old husband of thirty-five years. She also absolutely adored her only child, seeming to be unaware that her "child" was a thirty-three-year-old doctor. "Jeff, dear, are you sure I can't get you anything else to eat? You're not still hungry?"

"Thanks, Mom, but I can't eat another bite. Believe me, four eggs, six slices of bacon, half a cantaloupe and three slices of toast is a perfectly adequate breakfast." Jeff rolled his eyes comically at Autumn as he spoke fondly to the woman hovering over his chair.

His mother refilled his coffee cup for the third time, then dropped a kiss on his cheek. "Just let me know if you need anything else, you hear? What about you, Autumn? More bacon? Toast?"

"No, thank you, Mrs. Bradford, I'm fine." Autumn smiled a bit weakly at the woman with Jeff's blue eyes peering anxiously at her from beneath impeccably styled salt-and-pepper hair.

"Now, Autumn, I've told you to call me Kathleen. Mrs. Bradford is much too formal for family."

Autumn's smile grew weaker. "All right. Kathleen."

"Got any more of that fresh-squeezed orange juice, hon?" Charles Bradford asked, setting aside the morning newspaper he'd been scanning during breakfast, though it hadn't kept him from contributing occasion-

ally to the lively conversation that had gone on between his wife and son. Autumn had been rather quiet
during the meal, watching the interplay between the
Bradfords, while she'd made every effort to be polite.
She and Jeff had left Tampa early that morning to join
his parents for breakfast on their anniversary morning, and they planned to stay through lunch the next
day.

Kathleen bit her lip in obvious dismay at her husband's request. "No, we drank every drop. But I'll go
make some more," she added hastily, hurrying toward
the kitchen.

"That's okay, Kathleen. You don't have to—"

But she was already gone, her activities conveyed to
them by a flurry of sound from the kitchen. Charles
turned an amusingly wry smile at his son, who returned the look with a low laugh. "You've set her off
again," Jeff accused his father.

"Guess so." Charles looked across the table at Autumn, clearly feeling it necessary to entertain his guest,
though he seemed to be a somewhat shy man to whom
casual conversation did not come easily. The successful businessman was lean and fit, darkly tanned, and
Autumn could easily tell where Jeff had gotten his
movie-screen handsome looks. Only the blue eyes had
come from Kathleen; other than that, Jeff was the image of his hazel-eyed father. "How long have you been
an electrician, Autumn?"

Autumn glanced quickly at Jeff, remembering the
moment he'd asked her the same question. His smile
told her that he, too, remembered. "Five years," she
answered his father's question.

"You really like it?" Charles looked doubtful.

She smiled at him, amused by his expression. "Yes, sir, I really like it."

Charles shook his head once. "I never was any good with that kind of thing myself. The boy here's just like me. Not mechanical. Last time I tried to do anything electrical, I just about electrocuted myself."

"The boy" grinned and added, "I did the same thing when I was trying to fix a television set once. Forgot to unplug it." He winced good-naturedly and added, "I haven't touched anything electrical since, other than to plug it in and turn it on or off."

Autumn laughed softly. "I've been shocked a few times," she admitted. "And to be honest, I *hate* to be shocked. Fortunately, I've never been badly hurt."

"So how long you planning to do this sort of thing?" Charles inquired curiously.

Autumn lifted a questioning eyebrow. "I beg your pardon?"

"The electrical work," Charles explained. "You planning to stay with it awhile longer, or is there something else you want to do?"

"I like my job," Autumn told him again. "I have another year before I can test for my master's license, and then maybe I'll start my own company someday. That won't be for several years, though."

Charles frowned, obviously trying to understand her. "But what if you were to marry, have children?" he asked with a sidelong glance at Jeff.

Jeff interceded quickly. "Dad, lots of wives and mothers work these days. Most of them, in fact. And not all for financial reasons. Many women work because they feel the need to establish their own identities outside the home."

"I never felt that way myself," Kathleen commented, entering the room with a full pitcher of fresh-squeezed juice. "I was perfectly content making a nice home for my husband and my son. And I was always busy in community activities," she continued with a smile at Autumn. "It's nice to stay involved in the community."

"Women used to think that was enough," Charles mused, glancing from Autumn to his wife as if comparing the two very different generations sitting at his breakfast table. "For thirty-five years Kathleen's been at my side, taking care of our home. She was there for Jeff when he came home from school, room mother for his classes, den mother for his Boy Scout troops. Yet I never doubted that she had her own identity."

"Now, Charles, this isn't the time for one of your discussions about the changing times," Kathleen reproved him indulgently. "You have women on the management staff of your own company, and you're known as an equal-opportunity employer. What was right for me isn't necessarily right for everyone, and neither of us is saying it should be."

"That's true," Charles confessed. Still, he couldn't seem to resist one more question on the subject to Autumn. "Did your mother work while you were growing up?"

"No, she didn't," Autumn admitted uncomfortably. "Except to help Daddy out with his store occasionally."

"Autumn's father owns a seed and feed store in Rose Bud, Arkansas," Jeff inserted, smoothly changing the subject. "That's close to Greer's Ferry Lake, Dad. Remember the time we went camping there with Uncle Dan and Aunt Josie?"

Charles nodded. "Good fishing lake. Beautiful scenery, too. My brother was career Air Force," he explained to Autumn. "Retired at the Little Rock Air Force Base in Jacksonville. He and his family liked it so well they stayed. Still live there."

"Jacksonville's not far from Rose Bud," Autumn commented, relieved that the topic had changed so easily and grateful to Jeff for engineering it. "Jeff told me he had family in Arkansas. Quite a few Air Force people end up staying when they're stationed there."

And then the conversation carried on for a time along those lines, contrasting the similarities and differences between Arkansas and Florida and the pros and cons of living in either state. But Autumn couldn't quite forget the earlier discussion, nor could she help but notice how diligently Kathleen Bradford waited on her "menfolk." Though Jeff seemed indulgently amused by his mother's attentions, and made no effort to encourage her, Autumn couldn't help wondering if he really enjoyed all that flattering attention.

After breakfast Kathleen refused to allow either Autumn or Jeff to help with the dishes but insisted that Jeff show Autumn around. Knowing of her fascination with the circus, Jeff took her to the thirty-eight-acre estate of the late John Ringling—of Ringling Brothers and Barnum & Bailey Circus fame—who, in 1927, had made Sarasota the winter headquarters for his circus. There they toured the Ringling Residence, a thirty-room mansion resembling a Venetian palace, completed in 1926 at a cost of one and a half million dollars. Hand in hand, they also toured the John and Mable Ringling Museum of Art, built in Italian Renaissance style and housing an impressive collection of fourteenth- to eighteenth-century art, and then—Autumn's favorite—the Museum of the Circus.

They had a wonderful time, neither of them referring to the briefly uncomfortable scene at the breakfast table. Autumn didn't know if Jeff avoided the subject because it bothered her or because he wasn't aware of how much it *had* bothered her.

They visited his parents again during the late afternoon, then went to the separate rooms they'd been assigned—without protest from Autumn, who wouldn't have expected to sleep with Jeff in her parents' home, either, despite her usual distaste for hypocrisy—to change for the anniversary party.

Autumn had bought a new dress for the occasion on a shopping trip with Emily, who'd also bought a new dress for a special date with her now-steady escort, Webb. Autumn's dress was a soft green, accenting her auburn hair and emerald eyes. The sleeves were long and the scooped neck quite modest, but still the garment managed to be seductive. Made of silk, it clung lovingly to her curves, making the most of her full breasts and tiny waist. She added black heels, then stared doubtfully into the full-length guest-room mirror, wondering if she'd made the right choice.

"You are so beautiful." Jeff's hoarse voice took her by surprise; she hadn't heard him come into the bedroom.

She turned and looked at him, tempted to echo his words as she took in his finely tailored dark suit that emphasized his muscular fitness so nicely. "You shouldn't be in here with the door closed," she told him with mock sternness, ordering her heart to stop fluttering so wildly. "You'll shock your mother."

"Then we won't tell her," he answered, stepping closer. "New dress?"

"Yes." She turned slowly for him. "Like it?"

"Very much." He slipped his arms around her. "And I love you."

Autumn's arms closed around his neck in a sudden rush of near desperation. "I love you, too, Jeff," she told him in a voice that surprised even her with its raw intensity.

"Autumn." He kissed her deeply, roughly, then held her a few inches away. "Is anything wrong?"

"No." She shook her head determinedly. "No, nothing's wrong. I just felt like telling you that I love you."

"I'm glad." His smile was spine-melting. "You don't say it enough."

"Don't I?" she asked without returning the smile.

Sensing that she'd meant the question seriously, he lifted one hand to her cheek, keeping the other arm around her to hold her close. "You could say it with every breath and I wouldn't hear it enough," he told her, his voice deep and so very sincere.

And then the hand on her cheek moved to bury itself in the glossy hair at the back of her head, his mouth coming down on hers with a hunger that never seemed to be abated, no matter how many times they were together. Autumn understood, since her own desire for him was as fresh and piercing as it had been from the first time he'd kissed her.

Long minutes later Jeff laughed raggedly under his breath and set her firmly away from him. "We'd better stop this or we *will* end up shocking my mother," he muttered regretfully. "Are you ready to go?"

"Give me a couple of minutes to repair my makeup and I'll join you downstairs," she answered unsteadily after swallowing to clear her throat.

He nodded, kissed her swiftly one more time, then left her to scowl despairingly at the tousled, starry-eyed woman in the mirror.

Autumn's concerns about people misinterpreting her relationship with Jeff proved justified at the anniversary party held at a local country club, of which Jeff's parents were members. Jeff was well-known by his parents' friends, most of whom had known him since he was a toddler, and they'd apparently been hoping to see him married off for some time. Though he continued to introduce her quite correctly as "my friend, Autumn Reed," he might as well have added "the woman I love and want to marry," Autumn thought in exasperation. Something in his expression or his voice or his eyes when he said her name made people smile indulgently at her and all but pat her cheek with delight.

"So you're Jeff's little lady," one portly, red-nosed gentleman boomed loudly, making Autumn have to fight a wince. "It's about time that boy found himself a mate. And aren't you a pretty little thing?"

"It's so sweet to see the smile on Jeff's face when he looks at you," a blue-haired older woman told her later. "You make such a cute couple."

"You're an electrician?" one Junior League-type society matron exclaimed in near horror after a brief conversation with Autumn when Jeff had been pulled away by his father and another man. "At least you'll be able to get away from that when you marry Jeff. A doctor is such a nice catch, don't you agree?"

"How are you holding up, honey?" Jeff asked sympathetically as they grabbed an opportunity to converse with each other on the dance floor.

"Are you aware that, as we speak, two-thirds of the population of Sarasota is watching us dance with sickly sweet smiles on their faces?" Autumn demanded in low-voiced frustration, holding on to her party smile with great effort. "I have been called 'little lady,' 'a pretty little thing' and 'dear girl.' I've been told that you and I make a 'cute couple' and that you're a 'nice catch.' I've heard about all the women who've 'set their caps' for you, and all the 'matchmaking mamas' who've wanted you to marry their daughters. I've been asked if I was aware of the demands made on a doctor's wife, and wasn't I glad that I wouldn't have to work at manual labor once I have you to support me. One woman even asked if twins run in my family."

"Well, do they?" he asked with a not-very-well-concealed smile.

Her answer was short, succinct and would have appalled all the little old ladies smiling so approvingly at her from around the room had they heard the murmured words. Jeff laughed aloud, causing those smiles to broaden. "So," he managed to say when he'd caught his breath, "how are you enjoying the party?"

In the same deadly quiet voice she told him exactly what he could do with his party and with his amusement, making him laugh again. "I can't resist this," he told her, then kissed her thoroughly, right in the middle of the dance floor, to the delight of their enthralled audience. "I love you," he told her when he released her mouth, making no effort to prevent anyone else from hearing him.

Fortunately for him, the dance ended just then—before Autumn could deliver the embarrassing and rather painful retribution that she was seriously considering. He wrapped an arm around her waist and led her to the buffet table to join his parents, effectively blocking any further conversation between them. For the rest of the evening they mingled, and Autumn was able to maintain her politely bland facade, never once revealing her true feelings as she had to Jeff on the dance floor. Though she seethed at his amused response to her complaints, she didn't know what she'd really expected from him. It was so easy for Jeff to shrug off other people's comments or attitudes, she thought almost resentfully. He was an exceptionally tolerant man, able to talk pleasantly to others despite differing viewpoints. But then again, no one had called him a "pretty little thing," she fumed.

"OKAY, AUTUMN. Let's talk about it. What's wrong?" Jeff demanded when they were alone in her apartment the next afternoon, having carried in Autumn's things from Jeff's car and retrieved Babs from Emily.

"Nothing's wrong, Jeff," she lied composedly, avoiding his eyes as she stroked the dog in her lap. "Did you miss me, Babs?" she murmured, trying to ignore Jeff's dissatisfaction with her answer. "Were you a good girl for Emily?"

Sighing audibly, Jeff lifted the dog from Autumn's lap, set her on the floor with an affectionate pat and settled firmly on the couch beside Autumn. "I'm not letting you change the subject this time," he informed her decisively. "You've pulled back from me emotionally again, and I want to know why. You can start by looking at me. I don't think you've really looked at me all day."

She kept her eyes trained steadily on her hands, laced in a white-knuckled grip in her lap. She'd known this confrontation was coming, but she hadn't been looking forward to it. She'd known it was inevitable since that kiss on the dance floor the evening before. It had been late when they'd returned to Jeff's parents' home, and there had been no chance for the two of them to be alone since, other than during a lingering good-night kiss before retiring to their separate beds. Autumn had carefully avoided his eyes through breakfast, church services and lunch with his parents and, claiming weariness from a night spent in unfamiliar surroundings, had feigned sleep during the drive back to Tampa. Jeff had allowed her to get away with the postponement efforts—until now. He would wait no longer for his explanation.

She'd made a decision during the long sleepless night in the guest bedroom of the Bradford home. She hadn't cried when she'd come to the painful conclusion, but she'd felt her heart twisting into knots in her chest. Still, she had to do it, she told herself relentlessly. It was the only decision she could make that was fair to both Jeff and her. "I think we should stop seeing each other, Jeff," she said, her voice entirely devoid of emotion.

He went very still beside her. "You think *what*?" he asked quietly.

"I'm sure you heard me," she replied, still looking down at her hands. Part of her mind wondered absently if her knuckles could get any whiter.

"Oh, I heard you," he agreed flatly. "I'm just not sure you really meant it."

"I meant it." She dipped her head a bit lower, her hair falling forward to partially hide her face. "There's no future for us, Jeff. If we keep seeing each other, one of us—or both of us—will be hurt. I'd like to avoid that."

"I'm sure you would." His voice held more sarcasm than she'd ever heard from him. She risked a quick glance at his face, then quickly turned her eyes back downward, not liking what she'd seen. "Want to tell me what precipitated this?" he asked with polite detachment. "I was under the assumption that we love each other. As a matter of fact, you told me only yesterday that you love me."

"I do love you, Jeff," Autumn whispered. She strengthened her voice. "But you've known all along that I wasn't looking for permanence. I told you that I wasn't cut out for marriage. I just can't be any man's 'little woman.'"

"That is utter garbage and you know it. Tell me, Autumn, what was it that caused this grand decision of yours? A few tactless remarks at the country club? Something my parents said at breakfast yesterday? Something *I* said?"

The hint of pain behind the bitterness went straight to her heart. She'd give anything not to hurt him. But, being Autumn, she reacted to her own pain and confusion by lashing out in anger. "Stop patronizing me, Jeff!" she snapped, jumping to her feet and finally turning to face him. "Stop acting like I don't know my own mind. This has been building for weeks. The weekend only convinced me of what I had to do."

"Suppose you elaborate a bit." His face was hard, his jaw set ominously. She'd never seen him look quite so . . . intimidating.

"I'm feeling smothered again, Jeff," she told him in a rush of words. "Just like last time, with Steven." She had to look away from the expression that crossed his face when she compared him to her former fiancé. "I can't give you what you want, Jeff. I can't give up the independence that I've worked so hard to attain to try to make you happy."

"I have never," he told her concisely, rising to his feet, "asked you to give up anything. I want to marry you,

Autumn, not chain you to a bed or a stove. I want us to share our lives with each other, not sacrifice our lives for each other. Is that so damn much to ask?"

"Yes!" she shouted. "It is! I don't know *how* to be a wife, Jeff! I don't know *how* to be a mother. Dammit, I don't even know how to be a lover. I only know how to be myself, Autumn Reed."

"That was all I ever wanted you to be." His voice was low, throbbing with pain.

"But how long would you be satisfied with that? How long would you be happy with a wife who wears coveralls and hard hats to work? Who sometimes comes home with bruises or cuts from work-related injuries? Whose friends all wear blue collars to their jobs? How long before you start asking me to behave like a proper physician's wife, join the right clubs, cultivate the right friends? Give you the same kind of Ozzie-and-Harriet-Nelson-Ward-and-June-Cleaver relationship your parents have?"

Autumn had once wondered if it was possible to make Jeff lose the temper he'd once warned her about. It was.

"How dare you?" he demanded, his hands falling ruthlessly onto her shoulders, his grip anything but gentle. His blue eyes were blazing, his handsome face set in white-mouthed fury. The fine tremor in his fingers let her know that he really wanted to shake her, hard, but he restrained himself. "Who the hell do you think you are to criticize my parents? And just what gives you the right to tell me what *I* want or need from a wife?"

He snatched his hands away from her as if he couldn't bear to touch her for another minute, shoving them violently into the pockets of his jeans. "All right, Au-

tumn, if you want honesty, then you're going to get it.
You are a spoiled, self-centered, immature, frightened
child. You put on a big act of being sophisticated and
liberated, when the truth is that you're a young woman
from small-town Arkansas who hasn't got the guts to
take emotional risks. You don't seem to be afraid of
physical risks or physical pain, but you run like hell
from any kind of mature, responsible relationship. Not
because you don't want it, Autumn, but because you're
too damn scared you can't handle it!"

Feeling the blood drain from her face at his words,
Autumn gasped, furious at his unprecedented attack.
"Why, you—"

Jeff kept on as if she hadn't made a sound. His jerky
movements indicated just how little in control of himself he really was, despite his bitingly concise, low-
voiced words. "You're not the liberated woman you
want to be. You're chained to a lot of old fears and insecurities that trap you in a lonely, unfilled life, despite
your claims that you're perfectly happy alone."

Wanting to lash out at him as he was at her, Autumn
tried to interrupt, but he was on a roll, spurred on by
sheer rage, and he wasn't finished.

"When I came along, I didn't try to change you. I love
you exactly the way you are, stubborn and fiery and
self-reliant and all. But you had to start looking for new
excuses to break it off because you're still afraid to become deeply involved."

Though temper still edged his voice and hardened his
face, his eyes suddenly looked sad. "So now you think
you've found the perfect excuse. Not that I *have* tried
to change you, but that I *may* try to change you at some
nebulous point in the future. I've got to admit it's a great
accusation, Autumn. One I can't disprove because I

have only my word that I would never want you to change. And that's not enough for you, is it?"

"No!" she almost screamed, then made a deliberate effort to lower her voice and regain her tenuous self-control when it appeared that he was actually going to allow her to say a few words. "Maybe you think now that you don't want to change me, but how do you *know*? You could change your mind in a year or two years or five. How could you possibly know that you won't?"

"I know because I know myself," he replied flatly. "Unlike you, I don't try to deceive myself or others about what I want, what I need. I love you now, just as I'll love you in a year or two years or five. Or fifty. And you're willing to just throw that love away because you're too scared to take the risk that everything won't always be perfect. Too selfish to be willing to make a few compromises to smooth the way during the rough times."

His words hurt. Deeply. And they made her even angrier. She wanted to hurt him as badly, but instead of the insults that hovered on her tongue, a quiet question came out. "You can say all these things about me and still claim to love me?" she asked him, her voice strained, tight.

"I don't *claim* to love you. I do love you. Exactly the way you are. And you're not perfect, Autumn. Neither of us is." He pulled one hand out of his pocket to run a weary hand through his hair. "I'm going to spell this out for you one more time, and then I'm going to leave you to decide once and for all what you want for us. I love you. I want to marry you. I want to have children with you. I don't want to change you. If I wanted to be pampered and waited on and catered to, I'd move back home to my mother. I love her deeply, but being treated like a five-year-old drives me crazy. Why do you think I moved to Tampa? I can see my parents when I want to, but I'm far enough away that I can live like a real grown-up the rest of the time.

"I was never looking for a wife who'd subjugate herself to me, Autumn. I want a mate, a partner. Someone to stand beside me, not behind me. I want *you*, Autumn. Only you. I'm willing to make every sacrifice, every compromise I have to make to have you. But only if you're willing to do the same. You think about it. If you decide I'm worth the effort, you know where to find me."

And then he kissed her, hard, not giving her a chance to respond even if she had wanted to. Almost blind with atavistic pain and fury, she jerked away from him. And he left her, standing in the middle of her living room floor and staring at the door he'd closed much too softly behind him.

Autumn spent the next hour throwing pillows, storming around the apartment in a temper tantrum. Remembering every terrible word he'd said, every slashing accusation.

"He's an idiot," she told Babs, pacing like a madwoman. "Everything he said was garbage. After all this time he doesn't even know me! But he sure as hell thinks he does!"

She paced and raged and muttered until the early hours of morning, when she finally threw herself onto her bed, physically and emotionally exhausted.

And then she cried. For a very long time.

SHE HADN'T KNOWN that anyone could hurt so much and for so long and still continue to function. The passage of almost three long weeks did nothing to assuage the pain of ending her relationship with Jeff. Webb's proud announcement that he was making Autumn foreman of a large, upcoming job should have made her happy. It brought her no joy at all. Only a dull ache because she had no one to tell her how proud he was of her accomplishment.

Webb's rather sheepish announcement a few days later that he and Emily were engaged almost destroyed her. She made a valiant effort to look happy for him. "I told you you were marriage bait," she said in a weak attempt at teasing.

"I guess you were right," he admitted with a grin, not looking at all chagrined at being proven wrong. "I was always against marriage in the past because I hadn't met Emily yet. I guess I was just waiting for her all along."

"You're absolutely sure that you want to do this?" Autumn asked him searchingly, envying his calm certainty.

"I'm absolutely sure," he answered without a moment's hesitation. "I love her, and I love Ryan, and I want to spend the rest of my life with them. So go ahead, Autumn. Make fun of me all you like."

"No," she whispered, her eyes filling with tears. Horrified, she tried to hold them back. She hadn't cried in front of anyone in more years than she could remember.

But Webb saw the tears and took her in his arms. "I'm sorry you're hurting, Autumn," he murmured, his voice deep with sympathy. "Isn't there anything I can do to help? Can't you and Jeff work out your problems somehow?"

"I drove him away," she said with a sob. "I took everything he offered and threw it away. And I'm afraid it's too late to get it back."

"It's not too late. It can't be. The man's in love with you, Autumn."

"He deserves someone better," she murmured, burying her face in Webb's comforting shoulder. "Someone who's not afraid to take risks," she added, remembering all those painful, heated, and oh-so-true accusations Jeff had made. Now she understood what Spring had meant that day in Little Rock. Spring had claimed to know her sister was in love because Autumn was worried about not being good enough for Jeff. Now Autumn understood.

Webb tried to talk to her further, offering again to help, but she drew back, wiping her eyes and forbidding him to mention the subject again or to contact Jeff. She apologized to him for casting a pall on his own happiness and forced herself to smile and talk about his wedding plans, trying to ignore the continuous pain the subject brought her. Webb wasn't satisfied, but he knew her well enough to accept that the subject was closed. Permanently.

12

ON SUNDAY, three weeks after the day she'd sent Jeff away, Autumn took a long look at herself in the mirror and knew that she couldn't go on running. Perhaps she'd been quite content with her life prior to meeting Jeff. But she *had* met him and she'd fallen in love with him, and living without him was destroying her. So now it was time to decide exactly what it was that was keeping them apart, why she was afraid to share her life with him when she loved him so very much.

Need. It all came down to need. She was so afraid to admit that she needed him. But she did. She needed him desperately, and there was no way she could continue to deny that very obvious fact. Loving someone was thing, but needing someone was terrifying. What happened if she needed someone who was no longer there for her?

On a sudden impulse she picked up her telephone and dialed Spring's number. She didn't even identify herself when Spring answered but blurted out a blunt question. "Spring, what would you do if something happened to Clay, or if he left you?"

Spring paused for a moment, then asked for clarification. "What would I do?"

"Yes. You have your career, you'll have your child in late July. Would those things be enough to make you happy if you lost Clay? I know this is weird, Spring, but humor me, will you?"

"They wouldn't be enough," Spring replied, making an effort to answer honestly. "I love my work and I'll love my child, but Clay is a part of me. Without him that part of me would die. Oh, I'm not saying that I would literally die, though I might want to at times. I'm sure that life would go on, and perhaps I'd even find peace after a time. But I'd never be whole again. Do you understand that?"

"You need him," Autumn said with a sigh.

"Yes. I need him. I need him to make me laugh and keep me from being too serious about life. To be there for me when I need a hug or encouragement. To talk to about anything and everything that interests us. To make love with. And Clay needs me, too. For moral support when he's having a hard time getting through to one of his patients, to give him an outlet for the fears and vulnerabilities that he hides from others behind his funny clothes and quirky humor, to share the good times and the bad times. I don't spend time worrying about losing him, Autumn. I choose, instead, to treasure every moment I have with him."

"I don't want to need anyone," Autumn whispered starkly. "I don't want to know that part of me will die if I lose that person."

Spring's laugh was brief, gentle, understanding. "We don't choose to need, Sis. It's a part of living. When you love, you need." She paused, then asked carefully, "Are you and Jeff having problems?"

"We—I broke it off three weeks ago. I was afraid to make a commitment."

"I see. You were afraid that you needed him."

"Yes." The single syllable was painfully expressive.

"And do you love him any less now than you did three weeks ago? Does not seeing him take him out of your heart or your mind?" Spring asked wisely.

"No." Autumn dropped her head and closed her eyes, the receiver pressed close to her mouth. "No."

"Then you need him."

"Yes."

"The final decision is yours, of course, Autumn. I can't tell you what to do. But being afraid is such a paltry reason to throw away a chance for a lifetime of happiness, don't you think?"

"I don't know," Autumn admitted after a pause. "I honestly don't know."

"You know," her older sister answered confidently, "you only have to admit it to yourself, Autumn."

"I have to go, Spring. Thanks, okay?"

"Anytime. I love you, Sis."

"I love you, too." Autumn replaced the receiver, then almost immediately lifted it back to her ear, her fingers moving over the buttons to punch another often-called number.

"Hi, Summer, it's Autumn. I want to ask you a question, and I want you to answer honestly without asking why I want to know, okay?"

"Okay," Summer agreed easily. "Shoot."

"What would your life be like without Derek?"

"Empty. Lonely. Frightening." Summer answered without even hesitating. "Any other questions?"

"You were happy enough before you met him. You had a great time with your parties and your friends. You didn't need anyone."

"Wrong. I needed Derek. I just didn't know it until I met him. I may have been happy before without him, but I wouldn't be now."

"But he's so strong, so self-contained. Doesn't it bother you to need someone who doesn't need you as much?"

"Who says Derek doesn't need me? He does, Autumn. As much as I need him. He says I bring sunshine into his life, keep him from being a stuffed shirt. He claims that he was never really happy before I came into his life. Personally, I don't intend to argue with him. I'd rather believe him. Now do you want to tell me what this is all about?"

Autumn smiled tremulously. "I'm in love, Summer, and I'm scared witless about it. I guess I was just hoping that those of you who've been there and survived could pass along a few pointers."

"You want my advice about love? Grab on to it and hang on to it with all your strength. Because when it comes right down to it, there's nothing in life that's more valuable. And it's too rare to pass up once you find it. Does that make sense?"

"Oh, yes, it makes sense." Autumn pushed her hair out of her face and sent a smile through the telephone lines to her sister on the opposite side of the country. "I love you, Summer."

"I love you, too," Summer replied, surprised and pleased with Autumn's infrequent expression of affection. "Let me know how this comes out, will you?"

"I will. Give Derek a kiss for me. I'll talk to you again soon."

She spent the next hour on her couch, deep in thought, barely moving. Babs tried a few times to capture her attention, then gave up and curled up at her feet for a nap. Autumn thought about women she knew who hadn't been afraid of the risks—or if they had, they'd decided not to let their fear keep them from reaching for their happiness. Autumn's mother had chosen to give up teaching to raise her three daughters and sometimes help out in the store. Spring had combined a career in optometry with the responsibilities of being a wife and mother. Summer would finish her education soon and begin a new career but still looked forward to starting a family with her beloved, supportive husband. Jeff's mother seemed to truly enjoy taking care of her husband and her son, when he would allow her to do so. Jeff's friend, Pam, was a brilliant surgeon whose love for her accountant husband and baby daughter were evident to anyone who spent even a few minutes in her company.

Each of those diverse, intelligent women had deliberately chosen her path in life and had made whatever adjustments necessary to follow that path. No one had tried to tell Autumn that it was always easy, or that there hadn't been hard times, but all of them seemed content with their choices.

Autumn could marry Jeff and continue her career. He wouldn't ask her to give up her work or her plans for the future. He'd be right beside her, offering support when she wanted it, giving her freedom when she needed it. She finally allowed herself to acknowledge that it wasn't fear of losing her career or even her independence that had caused her to send him away. It was, after all, only a job.

So the crux of the problem was this need thing. And still she hadn't worked it all out. Some tiny detail was niggling at her, haunting her. Holding her back.

So deeply lost in thought was she that the telephone's strident ring made her jump and swear. She stared at it for a moment, wondering if it was Jeff. Just as she'd dreaded—and hoped—it would be Jeff every time someone had called during the past three weeks. "Hello?"

"Autumn? It's Pam Cochran."

Surprised, Autumn blinked and sat up straighter on the couch. "Hi, Pam, what can I do for you?"

"I'm calling about Jeff."

"Jeff?" Her heart suddenly stopped. "Is anything wrong? He's okay, isn't he?"

"No, he's not okay," Pam answered gravely, frightening Autumn even more. Her mind filled with all sorts of horrible possibilities as she broke into a cold sweat. And then Pam's words made her close her eyes in sheer relief. "He's miserable," Pam said flatly. "I've known him for a long time and I've never seen him suffer like this. What the hell is wrong with you?"

Light-headed with gratitude that nothing had happened to Jeff, Autumn chuckled weakly. "That's what I've been asking myself for a long time now, Pam."

"Look, I know this is none of my business, and he'd strangle me if he knew I was calling you, but I'm crazy about that guy and it's tearing me apart to see him this way. I'd stay out of it somehow if I hadn't seen the way you looked at him while y'all were together. I know you love him."

"Yes, Pam. I love him."

"So what's the problem? He needs you, Autumn. Why don't you go to him and put him out of his misery?"

He needs you.

Autumn promised Pam that she would make every effort to mend the damage to her relationship with Jeff, thanked her for calling and ended the call as soon as she could, her mind whirling with her revelation.

He needs you.

Clay needs me, too, Spring had said, not a trace of doubt in her voice.

Derek needs me as much as I need him, Summer had confidently assured her confused younger sister.

He needs you, Pam had said.

And now Autumn knew why she'd been afraid. Why she was still afraid. But suddenly she knew she had to try. Because she loved and needed Jeff Bradford.

AUTUMN HOPPED NIMBLY out of her Fiero, tugging the brim of her battered brown baseball cap low over her oversized sunglasses to shade her face from the Sunday-afternoon sun. Her auburn hair bounced defiantly around the shoulders of her yellow knit top as she strode briskly toward the front door of Jeff's house. She punched the doorbell with a slender, short-nailed finger, listening with satisfaction as the bell chimed inside.

The man who answered the door was as beautiful as ever, but three long, lonely weeks had left their mark on his handsome face. For the first time since she'd met him almost six months earlier, Jeff Bradford looked every year of his age and more. There were lines around his blue eyes that had not been there before, a grim cast to the mouth that had always smiled so easily for her.

She had hurt him deeply.

"Autumn!" Even his voice was different when he uttered her name, raw, hoarse, thick.

Autumn reached up to remove her sunglasses, revealing her eyes to him and hoping that he could read the love brimming in them. "I wouldn't blame you if you sent me away," she told him quietly, her own voice rather weak. "But I'm praying that you won't."

His knuckles were white on the edge of the door. "I guess . . . that depends on why you're here."

"I'm here to tell you that I've done what you asked. I thought about us, about what I wanted for us. And I've decided that I want it all. That you're worth the risks," she told him boldly, her gaze locked with his. "Please tell me you haven't changed your mind."

His eyes closed for a moment, then opened to bore into her. "Come in." He stepped back to allow her to pass him, being very careful not to touch her as she walked by. She longed to reach out to him, but she hadn't expected him to make it that easy for her. She understood. He had to be sure this time that she wouldn't hurt him again.

In his den she pulled off her cap and dropped it and her sunglasses on a table before turning bravely to face him. "I love you, Jeff," she told him before he could say anything.

Something that might have been hope rippled across his drawn face, but still he hesitated. "And?"

"And . . . I need you," she told him steadily. "I need you so desperately. Won't you please give me another chance?"

In answer he opened his arms, his beautiful face lighting with the smile that she had craved for the past three unhappy weeks. Autumn flung herself into those welcoming arms, her own going tightly around his neck.

"I'm so sorry, Jeff. So very sorry. I was an idiot."

"Yes, you were," Jeff agreed lovingly, pressing kisses along the curve of her cheek. "I missed you so much. I was afraid that you would manage to put me out of your life for good, that you'd never allow yourself to admit that you needed me in any way."

"I need you in every way, darling. And I'm not afraid to admit it now." She smiled tremulously up at him, her fingers stroking the silky dark hair at the back of his neck.

His eyes flared. "You've never called me that before. I like it."

"I'm glad." She tugged his head down to hers, and at last his mouth was on hers again. Their kiss was long and sweet and infinitely loving.

"Tell me why you were so afraid," Jeff urged her long minutes later, holding her close as they sat on his wood-framed couch. "Tell me what made you change your mind."

Autumn cuddled closer to his shoulder, one hand around his waist, the other stroking his chest. Desire was there, just beneath the surface of their contentment, but for now they needed this time to hold each other and talk. Time to heal the wounds they'd inflicted on each other.

"I don't know if I can put it into words," she murmured thoughtfully, trying to compose an answer that would make him understand the turmoil she'd gone through during the months since she'd met him. She tilted her head back against his arm to look at him as she spoke. "At first I was afraid of having to give up the freedom I've earned by being independent. I wasn't sure what I'd have to give up to take on the new role you offered me."

"I understand up to that point." Jeff stroked her arm almost absently, fingers lingering at the pink scar left from her accident some two months earlier. "Sex roles are confusing and frustrating, particularly the ones that are obsolete and ridiculously restrictive. Believe me, I know."

Autumn lifted a questioning eyebrow.

"I was always a guy who liked little kids," he explained with a slight smile. "When I was in high school, playing football and doing other macho things, I was still a sucker for babies and toddlers. You never saw me without a few younger kids tagging at my heels, imitating everything I did, taking everything I said as gospel. I loved the adulation, of course," he admitted with gentle self-mockery, "but more than that, I was fascinated by the way their minds developed and interpreted things. And I couldn't stand it when one of them got hurt."

"So you became a pediatrician."

"Yeah. It's perfectly acceptable now for me to like kids, but at the time I took a lot of ribbing. The other guys my age couldn't understand my affection for the little yard-apes, as they called them. It was okay for teenage girls to like children, but not teenage boys."

"I hadn't thought of that," Autumn admitted, struck by his words. He *did* understand. At least as much as a man could understand a woman's rebellion against society's restrictions.

"What I *don't* understand," Jeff continued, "is why I brought out such panic in you. From the beginning I accepted your career and never made demands on you to change. Couldn't you tell that I wasn't a rigid traditionalist, despite my traditional upbringing? After all, your own background was pretty traditional, and look at the way you turned out."

"I know. I was using that for an excuse," Autumn confessed, hanging her head. "I didn't realize it until the past few weeks. I wasn't really afraid of loving you or of you trying to change me. I was afraid of needing you."

He nodded. "I figured that out after you hurt yourself and you were so careful to point out that you would have been just fine without me. Were you afraid that you'd grow to need me and I'd let you down?"

"That's it, I guess. At first, I thought my fear of need was another facet of the man-woman thing. You know, not wanting to be one of those clinging, dependent women who needs a strong, dependable man to make her whole, to center her life upon. And maybe that *was* part of it. But today I finally understood what I was really afraid of."

"Which was?" he asked, going very still.

She squirmed around on the couch until she was facing him directly. "Don't you see? I didn't want to need you because I couldn't imagine that you really needed me." She raised a hand to silence him when he would have spoken impetuously. "No, listen, Jeff. You're handsome, popular, a successful pediatrician. You have many friends, a close family, a beautiful home. You could have any woman you wanted with very little effort. You seemed completely at ease with yourself and your life, happy and content. I couldn't see you needing me the way I was beginning to need you because I couldn't see anything missing in your life, any void I could fill."

Jeff had flushed uncomfortably at her matter-of-fact description of him. Now he shook his head in disbelief. "Really, Autumn."

She giggled a little at his embarrassment. "Oh, Jeff, I didn't realize that I had such an inferiority complex until I met you. I couldn't understand what a man like you could see in a semigrown-up tomboy. I was terrified that, just about the time I allowed myself to admit my love and my need for you, you'd wise up and decide that I had nothing to offer you."

"You *are* an idiot," Jeff told her in mock disgust, his gaze caressing her rueful face.

"I know that now. I've done a lot of thinking for the past few weeks. Today I started remembering a few times when you *did* need me. The time before Christmas when Julian paged you to tell you that the little girl with CF was dying. I didn't know how to reach out to you then, but I wanted to so badly. The time you lost the little boy in the car accident. The time you were up forty-eight hours straight and needed me to make dinner for us and then make sure you were allowed to sleep uninterrupted for eight full hours. The time your head hurt and I rubbed your temples for you. And I thought of all the many times I've needed you during the past few months and you were there for me. And I realized that *I* was the one who'd walked out. You'd allowed yourself to need me, and I wasn't there for you. I'm so very sorry, Jeff."

The last words were spoken in a thin whisper. Autumn's eyes had filled with tears as she thought again of how deeply she'd hurt him, how deeply she'd hurt both of them with her insecurities. One of those tears escaped to trickle down her cheek. She swiped impatiently at it.

Jeff caught her close, shaken by the tears. He'd never seen her cry, he realized in near awe. She'd never allowed herself to be that vulnerable to him before. Now he knew that everything was really going to work out. She was offering him all of herself. Just as she already possessed all of him.

"I love you, Autumn. I love you so much. And God knows that I need you like I've never needed anything before. I've always needed you. Don't ever send me away again. Please."

"No," she murmured brokenly, her damp cheek pressed tightly to his. "Never again. Do we have to talk anymore now, Jeff?"

"No, honey. No more talk for now." He stood abruptly, his movements sure and smooth as he lifted her high in his arms. "Let me show you how much I love you. How much I need you."

"Yes," she answered trustingly, smiling through her tears. "Show me, darling."

And though both of them knew she was strong and healthy and fully capable of walking, he carried her to his bedroom as if she were a rare, precious treasure. And she allowed him to do so, and gloried in the gesture, because she felt the same way about him.

It took several minutes to shed their clothing because both of them were trembling so hard that their fingers were clumsy and awkward. Jeff swore beneath his breath, then laughed shakily when the zipper of her jeans refused to cooperate. "Maybe you'd better do this," he told her unsteadily.

"Maybe I'd better," she agreed in tender humor and swiftly removed her remaining garments. Then she held out her arms to the beautiful, strong, vulnerable man that she loved.

Jeff kissed her deeply, falling with her to the bed, his hands feverishly reacquainting themselves with the soft curves he'd missed so desperately during the past weeks, that he'd been so afraid he'd never hold in his arms again. His breathing was ragged, his heart thudding frantically, and he had to pause and take a long, deep breath in an attempt to regain control. He felt like a nervous teenager, overwhelmed by the depths of his needs and emotions. He wanted to go slowly, to love her with skill and patience, to take her again and again to ecstasy before allowing himself his own relief.

But then Autumn's hands were on him, caressing, demanding, and he groaned and drove himself deeply into her, fiercely welcoming her cry of pleasure. Skill and patience were abandoned, control willingly relinquished, and they loved each other with all the passion and hunger inside them. Kissing, arching, rolling, panting. Gasping out their love and their pleasure. And when they reached the point where neither could postpone their climax, they shuddered together, their delirious cries echoing from the evening-shadowed corners of the room.

And then there was silence, except for their gradually slowing breathing. The shadows lengthened, spreading like a warm, soft blanket over the glistening, damp bodies entwined in the middle of the big bed. Peace was a living, palpable entity in the quiet room, guarding the doors against the outside world until the recuperating lovers were ready to face it. Together.

A very long time later—hours? days? eons?—Jeff's voice inserted itself smoothly into the silence. "Marry me, Autumn."

She smiled into his shoulder and wrapped herself more tightly around him. "Yes."

Nothing more. He held her even closer, his cheek against her hair, and together they drifted into the restful sleep they'd both been denied during the past three lonely weeks, knowing they'd wake still wrapped in each other's arms.

Epilogue

"I NEVER THOUGHT I'd see this," Summer Anderson said with an incredulous shake of her head, her short, honey-brown hair accented with a spray of miniature flowers, her brilliant blue eyes accentuated by her deep blue bridesmaid's dress.

"What makes *me* mad is that she had to let out the bodice of the dress," Spring agreed solemnly, the violet dress that matched her eyes styled to allow for her seven-month-plus pregnancy. She'd worn her silvery-blond hair up, and a spray of flowers identical to the ones Summer wore was clipped to one side. "Except for a slight difference in length, mother's wedding gown fit *us* just fine."

"Don't pay any attention to them, honey. You look just beautiful," Lila Reed told her youngest daughter with a smile as she straightened the antique-lace wedding gown Autumn had just slipped into. The dress clung snugly to Autumn's nice curves and fell to just above her ankles. Its tea-length design had made it quite convenient for all three sisters, who ranged in height from Summer's scant five-feet-four to Spring's five-seven.

"I feel kind of strange," Autumn admitted, observing herself in the mirror of the Bradford's guest room. The woman who stared back at her was a pink-cheeked,

dewy-eyed bride, her auburn hair twisted into a sleek
roll adorned with flowers. She looked small and feminine in the delicate lace gown. Autumn thought long-
ingly of her brown baseball cap and blue jeans.

She and Jeff had chosen to be married in the living
room of his parents' Sarasota home on this Saturday
afternoon in May. The guest list was small, somewhat
to Kathleen's disappointment. Kathleen had wanted an
enormous church wedding for her only son, to be attended by everyone she knew. Because the exchange of
vows would be such a deeply private moment for Autumn, she hadn't been able to comply with that request, but they'd compromised with this intimate, very
traditional ceremony to be followed by a reception at
the country club where the Bradfords had celebrated
their wedding anniversary a couple of months earlier.
Jeff and Autumn had agreed to attend the reception,
allow Kathleen to show them off a bit and then slip
quietly away for a week-long honeymoon in the Ba-
hamas, as neither of them could take off any longer
than that from their jobs.

"Daddy's waiting for you in the hallway," Spring told
Autumn, interrupting her bemused examination of her
reflection. "He's been grumbling all day about having
to go through this again, but he's really delighted that
he's going to have the chance to give away his remaining daughter."

Autumn muttered something about "archaic, sexist
traditions," but Spring only laughed and hugged her,
careful not to muss her. "You look happy, Autumn.
And Jeff is as wonderful as I'd expected him to be. I'm
so glad you managed to work out your problems."

"Thanks, in part, to you," Autumn answered gratefully, returning the hug. "You were so patient with me when I called you in hysteria."

"You'd have made the right decision without me," Spring answered confidently. "But I was happy to help."

Autumn patted Spring's protruding stomach. "You've got yourself a terrific mother, kid," she informed her soon-to-be niece or nephew.

"You'll make a terrific mother yourself," Spring returned, hinting broadly.

"Yeah," Autumn agreed happily. "I think I will."

Summer stepped up to claim her own hug, and then it was time for the wedding to begin.

Her hand held snugly in the crook of her father's arm, Autumn paused in the doorway of the flower-bedecked living room, taking a deep breath that strained the already-snug bodice of her mother's wedding gown. Her eyes rapidly scanned the small crowd of witnesses, her heart swelling with affection for each one. Webb, Emily and Ryan, already looking like a family, though the adults hadn't yet exchanged their own vows. Bob and Pam Cochran and their tiny daughter, Pam looking as proud as if she'd been entirely responsible for the happy outcome of Jeff and Autumn's romance. Derek and Clay, smiling fondly at their youngest sister-in-law. Autumn's mother and Jeff's mother, sitting side by side and sharing a box of Kleenex.

Finally Autumn's eyes lifted to the makeshift altar, where Jeff waited patiently for her, flanked by her sisters on one side, his father and his partner Julian on the other, the minister standing just behind him. Seeing him standing there, darkly handsome in his pearl-gray suit, his ebony hair gleaming in the overhead lighting, his blue eyes glowing with love and happiness, Autumn remembered the words that had come to her mind the first time she'd set eyes on him that morning in October. A beautiful man. Now she knew that he was as beautiful on the inside as he was on the outside.

Her gaze locked with his, she stepped confidently forward, perfectly content with the roles she had chosen. Wife. Lover. Partner. Friend. Jeff smiled and held out his hand.

HOURS LATER Autumn walked out of their hotel-room bathroom, her hair loose around her shoulders, the clinging black nightgown—a never-before-worn birthday gift from Summer—swishing around her ankles. She caught her breath as Jeff turned to smile at her, wearing only the bottom to a pair of gray cotton pajamas. "So you really do wear cotton pajamas," she managed lightly, her eyes drinking in the sight of his gleaming, lamplight-bronzed chest.

"I haven't worn them much since I met you," he admitted with a husky chuckle. "They always seemed unnecessary on the nights we spent together."

"So why are you wearing them now?" she asked softly, one eyebrow lifted meaningfully.

He hesitated for a moment, seeming to consider her question, then grinned and shrugged. "The same reason you're wearing that luscious gown, I suppose. A mere formality. Come here, Autumn Reed-Bradford."

Autumn laughed and went into his arms. "I think we can do away with the hyphen. I don't mind sharing your name. Perhaps the custom is obsolete, but it does make things less confusing in the long run."

"I love you, Mrs. Bradford," Jeff told her unsteadily, pulling her closer.

"I love you, Dr. Bradford." She lifted her face for his kiss.

Jeff started to walk with her toward the bed, but Autumn held back, shaking her head firmly. "Oh, no. Not yet. There's something you have to tell me first."

He grinned, knowing exactly what she meant. "Elwood."

Autumn choked. "Elwood? Your first name is *Elwood*?"

"*Harvey* was Mother's favorite movie," he explained diffidently, his cheeks suspiciously warm.

Autumn laughed so hard that she had to hold her side. "I knew you reminded me of someone. Jimmy Stewart as Elwood P. Dowd," she managed to say with a gasp. "The consummate gentleman, unfailingly polite and considerate. Gentle, kind, sensitive. Just naturally perfect."

"I'm not a lush!" Jeff protested. "I hardly drink at all."

Autumn waved a dismissive hand. "That's not what I was talking about, and you know it."

"I knew this is the way you'd react. That's why I refused to tell you before you married me," Jeff muttered, his lips twitching with the smile he was trying to hold back.

"Oh, Jeff, I love you." She threw her arms around him, causing him to lose his balance and fall backward onto the bed, his arms closing around her to catch her to his chest. "And I would have married you even if I'd known that your first name was Elwood. But don't you *dare* start talking to invisible rabbits!"

"I won't," he promised with a laugh, his hand going to the hem of her gown. In one smooth move he stripped the sexy garment off over her head, baring her to his exploration. The smile he gave her was anything but gentlemanly.

Delighted with the rare glimpse of the charming devil beneath his Southern gentleman exterior, Autumn abandoned herself willingly to her husband's love-making, eagerly returning the courtesy.

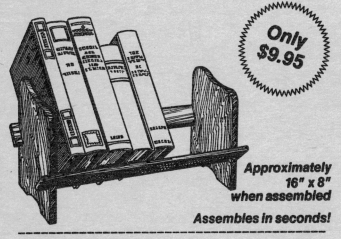

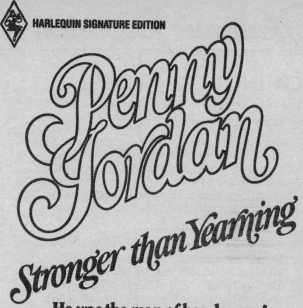

Harlequin Temptation

COMING NEXT MONTH